Murder & Misjudgment: A Pride & Prejudice Variation Mystery Romance

Crime & Courtship, Volume 4

Abbey North

Published by Abbey North JAFF Books, 2022.

Blurb

A trip to London promises to be exciting as Lizzy tries to help Jane find a way to meet with Mr. Bingley. Her own experience is enlivened by meeting Lord Aumley, a handsome young viscount thrust into the world of Society unexpectedly. She wants to like Lord Aumley as more than a friend, but when she sees Darcy again, she accepts she cares more about the prideful man than she should. Her heart seems set on him, though her mind is still resisting the idea.

While making it clear to the young viscount she has no interest beyond friendship, a homicide crosses her path, followed by another soon after. When Darcy notices the victims bear an uncanny resemblance to Lizzy, he swears to protect her—even if it means keeping her under lock and key. Lizzy isn't certain she's even at risk, but she wants to find the murderer in their midst while perhaps seeing unexpected changes in Darcy that lead her to contemplate his previous proposal with renewed attention.

This is part four of the "Crime & Courtship" series, which will be five books, intended to be read in order, and follow roughly the same timeline and location as J.A.'s masterpiece. The first mystery takes place in Meryton. The next will be at Netherfield, followed by Hunsford, then London, and finally Pemberley. The story arc will continue throughout all five parts, compromising one long read broken into five sections. A mystery is central to each installment, so you could call this a cozy mystery sweet Regency romance.

While Abbey sometimes writes sensual JAFF, this series is strictly SWEET.

Chapter One

Lizzy stood with Jane in the Perkins' drawing room, striving to have a good time. She'd been in London for a few weeks now, and while Aunt and Uncle Gardiner had been as warm and welcoming as ever, Lizzy felt vaguely discontent. She couldn't explain why, so she sought to divert herself from those emotions by throwing herself into every social activity available.

That was how she and Jane had come to accompany their aunt and uncle to this evening's rout-party at their friends' house. Now, Lizzy eyed the same people she'd been accustomed to interacting with for the past few weeks and felt the same swell of discontent. Something was missing, but she couldn't imagine what. She refused to speculate too.

"Did you receive a missive from Mary today?" asked Jane as she sipped a glass of lemonade.

Lizzy nodded, holding her own cup without bothering to lift it to her mouth. It was too tart for her tastes. "I did, along with letters from Mama, Kitty, and even a brief letter from Lydia."

Jane pulled a face. "Let me guess, the poor dear is dreadfully bored with the soldiers gone and being denied the opportunity to travel to London before the weather changed?"

Lizzy smiled. "You forgot she was unhappy with the gifts she received for Christmas."

"I do hope she can find a way to be content." Jane looked concerned. "It must be difficult for her, since she's such a vibrant and social creature, and with the soldiers gone, and us away, she has far fewer opportunities for frivolity."

Lizzy felt a surge of sympathy for her younger sister. "You are right. I was not as understanding as I could be. I must endeavor to write her back when we return to the Gardiners." Then she asked, "Why did you bring up Mary specifically?"

"She mentioned a young man named Jonathan Mayhew. Do you know him?"

Lizzy smiled. "I do, and so do you. He is Uncle Phillips's law clerk."

Jane's eyes widened, and she grinned in delight. "That is from where I know the name. Mary did not say much about him, only that he complimented her skills with the pianoforte when he came to dinner recently with others. I assume she must be referring to Aunt and Uncle Phillips."

Lizzy nodded. "I suspected she had a *tendre* for him based on their interaction the last time I saw them together, along with a conversation we had before the Netherfield ball."

Jane's expression looked pained then, and she said, "Excuse me. I believe I need more lemonade." It was a patent falsehood, for her glass was amply full, but Lizzy didn't call her on it. She knew Jane was still upset about the separation from Bingley, and she had yet to see him since her arrival in London.

Lizzy's lips curled with disapproval when she recalled Jane's recounting of calling on Caroline Bingley. The woman had pretended she was on her way out, and even Jane had questioned that. There'd been no question about Caroline's true friendship, and just how false it was, when she came to Gracechurch Street a few days later and made it clear to Jane she would never be acceptable to Bingley, and all hopes were pinned on Bingley and Georgiana making a match.

Lizzy's anger stirred anew, and she struggled to calm it. With Caroline actively thwarting them, she had no doubt Mr. Bingley didn't even know Jane was in London, and since they didn't move in the same social circles, she hadn't yet had an opportunity to see him. Lizzy had been trying her best to think of a way they could interact, or accidentally meet, but so far, she'd had no ideas.

Jane rejoined her just as there was a stir, and they turned to see what had caused the commotion. It appeared to be caused by the arrival of three guests, who were slightly late. They were all young men roughly around Jane's age, and Theodore Perkins, the son of Mr. and Mrs. Perkins, looked like he was puffed up from pride at their arrival. The young man was nineteen, and it was obvious he had a case of hero worship for whomever these new arrivals were.

Lizzy was curious herself as she eyed the three of them. One of the three was a rather portly young man with white-blond hair and a sickly complexion, but the other two were quite handsome indeed. At first glance, she thought they might be brothers, since they had similar builds and dark hair, but when she looked closer, she decided they were not related, at least not as closely related as she had imagined. "Who are they?" She asked the question of Jane.

"They are acquaintances of Theodore's," said Lily Perkins, hovering nearby. This Season was her first venture into society, and she still looked a little nervous. "I do not know much about them, for I have only seen them a few times, but I know the one in the middle is Viscount Aumley, and his name is Adam Turner. His handsome friend at his side is Mr. Tristan Nobles, and I believe the third gentleman is Mr. James Elliott."

"We have been graced with a viscount," said Lizzy with a minor twitch of her lips. "This must surely be the highlight of the Season." At least in the social circles in which they all moved.

Jane nudged her gently. "Be nice, Lizzy."

Lizzy gave her sister a bland smile. "I am being nice. I truly imagine it must be quite a coup for young Theodore to convince a viscount to show up at his parents' humble rout." She wondered what the viscount's angle was, but she didn't have long to await an introduction.

She found herself seated beside the viscount at the dinner table, with his friend Tristan across from them. Her immediate suspicion struck her as wrong after she'd had a few moments to converse with Adam, who seemed to be a captivating young man. Lizzy liked to consider herself above responding to superficial charm by now, but she couldn't deny he was a handsome man with a charismatic bent.

"What brings you here this evening, Lord Aumley?" asked Lizzy as their first course was whisked away. She felt slightly protective of Theodore, who was a naïve young man, and she hoped this wasn't some ploy to mock him or make him an object of jest.

"I quite like young Theodore," said the viscount, as though he'd read her thoughts. "I do wish you would call me Adam, Miss Bennet."

Her eyes widened. "I could not be that audacious, Lord Aumley."

He sighed. "No, I suppose you cannot. I admit, I am having some difficulty adjusting to my new role."

Her eyes widened as she buttered a roll. "What role is that, Lord Aumley?"

He tugged at his cravat, his finger dipping underneath the tight bow to loosen it. It almost seemed a subconscious gesture. "I never expected to inherit the title, I assure you. I was living in obscurity in Cornwall when I received the unexpected news that my great Uncle had died without another heir."

He pitched his voice low as he leaned closer, saying, "I was apprenticing to be a carpenter when I learned the news." There was a hint of gentle mocking in his tone, clearly directed toward himself. "Utterly shocking, is it not?"

Lizzy's lips twitched. "It is most appalling, Lord Aumley."

He sipped his wine before replying. "It was quite a scandal at first, so I shunned the *ton* last year upon inheriting the title. Duties in the House of Lords prevent me from seeking refuge this year. This is my first Season out, and I assure you, it still causes quite a stir when I move among the *ton*. There are those like young Theodore who look up to me, though I have scarcely done a thing to earn it, and there are just as many who are above me in status and wealth who look down upon me, recognizing me as the usurper I am." He sounded remarkably unconcerned about that.

"That must be difficult." She felt a stirring of sympathy for him, imagining how it was to suddenly be thrust into a higher echelon of society and be expected to easily adjust. Jane might have a similar issue if she ever married Mr. Bingley, but Jane was so kind and gracious that she could not imagine many people would be able to dislike her sister.

He seemed unconcerned. "As I said, it was an adjustment, and I am still making it, but when I contrast my existence now with what it was two years ago, I can hardly be displeased to have been so lucky. Fortunately, there are those who have been kind to me, like Tristan and James."

She smiled at Tristan, who looked at them when he heard his name. "That is a relief. Friendship does make burdens more tolerable."

Tristan's lips curved into a smile, making his rather thin face more appealing. "It has been my pleasure to be friends with Lord Aumley. Our acquaintance occurred at a timely fashion for me as well. I had just lost my fiancée in a terrible accident when we met, and Adam provided a good deal of distraction from the pain."

Lizzy's frowned. "I am so sorry." She didn't ask for details, though she was dreadfully curious. It wouldn't do to be poking and prodding into his pain though.

Dinner passed in a congenial exchange, though Tristan rarely contributed anything. He seemed to be on the quiet and shy side, but Adam more than made up for that. Lizzy was startled to realize she was thinking of him by his first name by the end of the meal. It was difficult not to. He had an open and friendly manner, and with his easy magnetism, she was predisposed to like him in no time.

There was nothing more to it than that, but when he suggested they sneak into the kitchen sometime later to have more of the delicious plum pudding, Lizzy and Jane found themselves agreeable to the idea. Jane was giggling, and so was Lizzy. She knew this was scandalous behavior, but it also sent a thrill through her, and since it seemed relatively benign, she didn't think they would have any problem.

They entered the kitchen a few minutes after, finding the staff still cleaning up from dinner. A young woman a few years older than Lizzy with dark brown curls and brown eyes looked at them. She seemed vaguely appalled for a moment before she remembered herself and curtsied. "How may I help you, misses and sirs?"

"We had hoped for a second helping of that delicious plum pudding," said Adam with a wink.

The woman blushed. "I made that." She announced it proudly, but still with a hint of modesty.

"It was exquisite," said Adam, sounding completely convincing.

Lizzy had no reason to doubt his honesty, for she had found it delightful as well. "It is probably the best one I have ever had, Miss...?"

She came out from behind the counter and approached them. "I am Marie Harris, the assistant cook. Cook has already gone to bed for the evening, but I do not believe he will mind if I slip you an extra serving. Nay, I doubt he will even notice."

"We do thank you, Miss Harris," said Adam as the assistant cook distributed small bowls to them moments later.

Jane eyed hers with clear trepidation. "It was so good, but I fear I might not have room for another serving."

"It certainly will not do you any harm," said Lizzy, admiring her sister's slender form. Lizzy was more on the curvy side, and though she knew she shouldn't indulge in a second serving, she plunged in her spoon without much regret. It was a delicious treat, and she happily surrendered her empty bowl a few minutes later, her stomach feeling far too full. "Thank you so much for your kindness, Miss Harris."

The girl curtsied. "Of course, miss. You are a guest in Mrs. Perkins's home, and anyone who likes my plum pudding deserves special consideration." She flushed as she laughed a little before taking Adam's bowl, and then Tristan's. Jane surrendered hers last, leaving a few bites behind. She seemed apologetic as she did so. "I am sorry. There is not a thing wrong with the plum pudding, but I have no more room."

"It is all right, miss."

After Marie had reclaimed their dishes, the four of them left the kitchen again and returned to company in the drawing room. Lizzy felt young and carefree in a way she hadn't for a long time, and she attributed that to Adam's influence and prompting them to do something so silly, yet harmless.

As they took seats on the settee, Adam and Tristan stood beside them, and Adam said, "You seem like an intelligent sort, Miss Elizabeth."

Lizzy flushed with pleasure at the compliment as she nodded. "I do like to think so. My papa would agree, but my mother would caution intelligence is an unattractive feature in a woman." She laughed slightly as she revealed the information, realizing it was probably too forward. She seemed like she was fishing for compliments.

His lips spasmed, and his brown eyes warmed further. "I am afraid I must disagree with your dear mother in that case. I have met a great many lovely young ladies during the Season thus far, but far too few of them are capable of holding a conversation. Have you been to the British Museum yet, Miss Elizabeth?"

She shook her head. "I have not yet had a chance to attend. Often when I am visiting my aunt and uncle, we have other duties and activities." Visiting the museum appealed to Lizzy, but it didn't seem the sort of entertainment the rest of her family would enjoy.

"I plan to attend tomorrow, wanting to see the Indian exhibit again. They do have quite a few fascinating relics, and information is readily available. If it would not be too forward, I would enjoy it if you attended with me?"

Lizzy blinked for a moment, hesitating. Was attending the museum a friendly gesture, or did he intend more? Was he laying the pathway to court her? Lizzy was more unsettled than pleased by the idea, though there was nothing wrong with the viscount himself. "I would like to do so. It is always lovely to make new *friends*, especially if they share common interests." She hoped she'd put just the right amount of emphasis on the word friends, not wanting to blatantly dissuade him, but also reluctant to allow him to believe there might be more to her interest than friendship.

He beamed. "Excellent. If you will give me your address, I shall call on you tomorrow at eleven to collect you and meet your guardians before we go to the museum."

Lizzy shared her address with him, and they settled into more generic topics of conversation. Lizzy found herself smiling more than she had in a while, and she finished out the evening with a pleasant glow of satisfaction as they returned to Gracechurch Street in the accompaniment of Aunt and Uncle Gardiner.

She and Jane went upstairs, going to the bedroom in the attic they shared while visiting. She helped Jane with unbuttoning her dress before turning so Jane could do the same for her. Aunt Gardiner had a lady's maid, but neither of them wanted to wait for Lucy to be finished helping her mistress, since they were both tired.

After sliding into her nightdress and getting onto her side of the bed, Lizzy curled up on her side, hugging the pillow and huddling under the warm blankets, since there was a chill in the room. Jane joined her a moment later, asking, "Do you like the viscount? He seemed quite taken with you, Lizzy."

Lizzy frowned, unaccountably thinking of Darcy's proposal for some reason before she banished the thought. "He seems like a nice young man. I think we might become friends, assuming we have enough common interests."

Jane giggled. "I would like for you to find someone who is more than a friend. Do you think that could be Lord Aumley?"

Lizzy hesitated before saying, "I do not believe so."

Jane sounded disappointed. "I am sorry, Lizzy. Surely, there is a man who will be able to please you at some point? I know you are committed to the path of spinsterhood, but I hope for you to fall in love." There was deep sadness in her tone then. "Not that falling in love guarantees happiness."

Lizzy turned, taking Jane's hand in hers in silent support. There was little she could say, but she hoped her presence alone was soothing as Jane wiped away a few tears before closing her eyes in a determined fashion, clearly intent on sleeping.

Lizzy closed her eyes as well, and she tried to think about the viscount she'd met that evening. He was a very handsome and nice man, but he didn't make her heart thump rapidly in her chest. Indeed, no man ever had.

As though her own conscience wished to call her a liar, the image of Fitzwilliam Darcy flashed behind her eyes, and her heartrate accelerated correspondingly. She gritted her teeth in annoyance with herself, doing her best to banish him from her thoughts so she could get a good night's rest before her outing with Lord Aumley in the morning.

Chapter Two

The viscount showed up at Gracechurch Street the next morning at eleven, precisely on time, which Lizzy found impressive. He made a favorable impression on her aunt, though Uncle Gardiner had already gone into work, so he wasn't there to meet him.

Once they had said their partings from Aunt Gardiner, and Adam had politely asked Jane if she would like to join them, though she refused, he led her to his black carriage, and she eyed the crest for a moment, noticing it had a gryphon. "It is lovely."

He frowned. "I find it all rather pretentious, to be honest, but I dare not change the family crest."

She put a hand to her mouth in mock-horror. "The very idea, sir. I am not certain I am safe with a man who would even think such a thing." She chuckled.

His expression softened, and he seemed to look at her with more than just friendly interest. She quickly schooled her features into a more serious arrangement, not wanting to encourage him to form a *tendre* for her. "I confess to being quite excited for our outing, Lord Aumley. I have wanted to visit the British Museum for years."

"I shall endeavor to ensure you enjoy your expedition then, Miss Elizabeth."

He was easy to talk to, and the minutes passed quickly as they made their way to the museum. His carriage drew up outside a short time later, and his driver opened the door for them. Adam emerged first and lifted a hand to assist her down, and then he tucked her hand on his arm as they walked up the steps, paid their admission, and entered.

Lizzy soon lost herself in a haze of happiness as she explored the museum. He was the perfect person with whom to attend, because he'd obviously been there before and knew some of the tidbits she didn't, and some that weren't revealed by the placards accompanying each exhibit, and he didn't grow impatient with her even when she lingered.

He had seemed to enjoy their visit as well, but he really lit up when they made it to the Indian exhibit, learning about the various spices and teas that were native to India, along with their caste system. She frowned in disapproval upon learning that widows were immolated with their dead husbands. "Ghastly."

Adam nodded his agreement. "Entirely. The poor dears should never have to suffer that way."

Most of what she learned was positive, but as they came to an exhibit about Kali, she was disconcerted to see a picture of the eight-armed goddess holding a human heart in one of her hands, and she appeared to be on the verge of eating it. "Oh, my."

There was a new note of excitement in Adam's tone now as he said, "Kali was a bloodthirsty goddess, and she demanded human sacrifice from her followers."

Lizzy frowned, feeling uneasy. "How barbaric."

He looked earnest as he nodded. "Entirely without a place in civilization, I quite agree, but it is fascinating, nonetheless. I like learning about religions, and I find it interesting how so many people could fall in line with the idea of sacrificing themselves or others to please their goddess."

"Religion can be a peculiar thing," said Lizzy, fearing she might come across as a heretic. "Even our own religion has some strange ideas, such as drinking wine as a substitute for the blood of Christ."

"I agree. The Catholics are similar, with the communion wafers that embody the body of Christ. It has its own roots in and is a form of cannibalism, I suppose."

Lizzy shuddered at the thought. "I would prefer not to think about that."

Adam laughed. "I can hardly blame you. If you are interested in the topic, I will be giving a talk about Kali at the Religious Antiquities Society near the end of the week. I would be pleased if you would like to be my guest. Since you are not a member of the Society, that is the only way you could attend."

Lizzy looked at the exhibit again, deciding it was intriguing enough, if unsettling, that she wanted to know more. "Yes, I do believe I would be interested, Lord Aumley."

He grinned. "Excellent. I shall endeavor not to bore you or the other members of the Society."

Lizzy put her arm through his again as they walked away from the Indian exhibit, heading toward the exit now that they had seen everything. "I find it impossible to believe you could bore anyone, Lord Aumley."

"Miss Elizabeth," said a cheerful young voice then.

Lizzy jerked in surprise before turning to find Georgiana Darcy in front of her. Her brother was at her side, and she gave Mr. Darcy a cool nod before bestowing on Georgiana a much brighter smile. "It is lovely to see you, Miss Georgiana. Are you a fan of the British Museum?"

Georgiana pulled a face, and she seemed to be pouting slightly. "Fitzwilliam insists it will further my education." She sounded pained.

"You must check out the Indian exhibit," said Adam in his enthusiasm for it, not waiting for a proper introduction. He seemed to realize what he had done, and he flushed as he fell silent.

Lizzy quickly introduced them, feeling sorry for Adam. He seemed to be settling well into his new role of viscount, but there were times when the working-class carpenter shone through. She was sympathetic toward it, but of course, Mr. Darcy seemed haughty and disapproving. That was hardly a surprise.

They chatted for a few moments before Georgiana said, "You must come for tea tomorrow afternoon, Miss Elizabeth."

Lizzy was tempted to refuse, but that was simply because she didn't want to spend more time with Fitzwilliam Darcy. He wasn't too likely to be there, and she was certain he would invent an excuse to avoid her company. After his audacious proposal, which she had soundly rejected, he was unlikely to want to spend any time with her either. She couldn't risk injuring Miss Georgiana's feelings, and she wanted to sit with the girl and have a genuine conversation, finding out what had happened after her abduction. "I would be pleased, Miss Georgiana."

The other girl smiled. "Excellent. I shall see you then, Miss Elizabeth."

Darcy was scowling heavily now, but his tone was moderate when he said, "We should tour the museum before it closes, Georgiana."

At his words, Lizzy looked at the clock on the wall, surprised to see it was after four. She hadn't realized she had lost track of time so thoroughly as she'd explored the museum.

Adam led her to his coach, and they were back at Gracechurch Street a few moments later. He walked her to the door and kissed her gloved hand in parting, saying, "I shall see you soon for the lecture."

"I am looking forward to it, Lord Aumley."

He bent at the waist as he stepped back. "Until we meet again, Miss Bennet." With those words, he turned and walked back to his carriage, where his driver held the door for him.

Lizzy entered the Gardiners' home, finding her aunt and Jane in the sitting room, both sipping tea and working on embroidery. "I apologize for being so late."

Her aunt seemed unconcerned. "I assumed you were having a splendid time at the museum. I have never been there, but I hear it takes many hours to fully appreciate."

"Indeed." Lizzy almost launched into a description of things she'd seen, but she curbed the impulse. She doubted Aunt Gardiner or Jane would have any true interest in the various items. She could well imagine their response if she told them a thing about Kali. It would turn them off the honey cakes and tea they were enjoying.

Instead, she sat down in the chair and said, "If it is all right, Lord Aumley has invited me to a lecture at his Society. There will be plenty of people there."

Aunt Gardiner looked up from her sewing. "I have no objection at all, my dear. I trust you to have sound judgment. Do you like this young man?"

Lizzy nodded. "He's a nice man. I believe we will be friends."

Her aunt frowned slightly. "Perhaps you will be more than friends?"

Lizzy shrugged. She didn't want to say a firm no, but she couldn't imagine growing that kind of affection for the man. Vexingly, Darcy's image returned to her mind once more, and she grimaced. She distracted herself by pouring a cup of tea and selecting a honey cake before returning to her seat. "I am not overly eager to marry, Aunt Gardiner."

Her aunt made a dismissive sound. "Some young girls think that, but you have only to meet the right man."

Lizzy almost choked on the honey cake in her mouth, using a fortifying gulp of tea to wash it down. "I find it difficult to believe such a rare and mythical creature might exist."

"Do not be so hard on the male sex," said Aunt Gardiner. "They are not as complex as women, and so you must give them allowances."

Lizzy thought that was an oversimplified and inaccurate assessment, but she didn't argue with her aunt. If it were true, it certainly wouldn't encourage her to want to make a match, for who would want to be paired with someone who was inferior to them?

For a moment, she wondered at Darcy's ability to overcome his own innate prejudices to offer for her. She moved uneasily in her seat, realizing perhaps she'd underestimated the depth of his affection for her if he were willing to overlook all her perceived flaws and offer anyway.

And yet how could she have seriously entertained the idea of accepting such an insultingly worded proposal, especially since he was still determined to keep Jane from Bingley? There was no time for second-guessing herself since the outcome couldn't be changed, and she assured herself she wouldn't want to anyway. The idea of marrying Fitzwilliam Darcy was preposterous.

Chapter Three

Lizzy slipped out of Gracechurch Street the next afternoon after discreetly informing her aunt where she was going. She'd been careful not to mention it in front of Jane, since Jane hadn't been included in the invitation, and Lizzy didn't want to spark her hope. She felt like she was sneaking around, but she had good reason to preserve her sister from the truth.

If she had a chance, maybe she would find a conduit to Mr. Bingley through her renewed friendship with Miss Georgiana, but she wasn't approaching the outing with that in mind. There was nothing nefarious about her friendship overtures toward the other woman. She genuinely liked Georgiana, and she didn't want to give her sister false hope.

She hailed a hansom cab, and it dropped her in front of Darcy House a while later. Lizzy swallowed at the sight of it, daunted by its obvious luxury. The house could easily hold her aunt and uncle's abode several times over.

She straightened her shoulders, determined not to be intimidated, and approached the front door. The butler opened it a moment later, and his lip curled with obvious displeasure. Lizzy knew there was nothing wrong with her attire, though her dress was not the most expensive fabric, so she couldn't help hoping he had that same reaction to all guests. Likely, he considered everyone beneath the Darcys.

"I have an appointment for tea with Miss Georgiana."

He seemed shocked by that, but he inclined his head. "You must be Miss Bennet?" At her nod, he stepped back and opened the door. "Please come in and follow me."

Lizzy did so, following the dour butler through the halls, deciding she would need a map to navigate her way around if she hadn't had his assistance.

He led her into a sitting room, and she was happy to see Georgiana, though dismayed to see Darcy had joined them. She managed a cool nod in his direction, and then her smile brightened again when she saw Mr. Bingley sitting on the settee. She found herself sitting beside him moments later after they had exchanged greetings. "I did not expect to see you here, Mr. Bingley."

He frowned. "Indeed, I did not expect to see you either. I had no idea you were in London. I simply dropped in to visit Darcy, and Miss Georgiana invited me to stay for tea."

"Miss Georgiana is quite perceptive," said Lizzy with a smile in her friend's direction. "She must have realized I would be happy to see you."

"Likewise," said Mr. Bingley, though he was fiddling with his spoon in a nervous fashion. He seemed to be gathering his courage when he said, "I hope your family is well."

"Quite well. Poor Lydia is quite bored without Jane and I there to keep her company though," said Lizzy smoothly, hiding her smile behind her sip of tea when she saw how Darcy stiffened at the mention of her sister's name.

Bingley had stiffened as well, but his expression was one of eagerness rather than irritation. "Miss Jane is here in London?"

Lizzy nodded. "She has been for a few weeks. I joined her after my visit to Hunsford. Mr. Darcy might have mentioned our visits overlapped, as he was there to see his aunt?"

Bingley frowned. "He mentioned nothing of the sort, and he did not tell me Jane was in London either." He was openly glaring at his friend.

Darcy shrugged a shoulder. "It had slipped my mind, Bingley."

Lizzy's eyes narrowed as she also glared at him. "I am certain of that," she said while making little attempt to hide her disbelief.

"I wonder why Miss Jane has not called at Grosvenor Street," said Bingley with a frown.

Lizzy proceeded carefully, not wanting to cause a scene, but she refused to allow Mr. Bingley to believe Jane hadn't been interested in him and hadn't come to see him. "She did shortly after her arrival, but Miss Bingley made it clear she was not welcome there."

Darcy stiffened, his anger tangible as Charles gasped.

"That cannot be. There must be a mistake, for my sister and Miss Jane were friends."

"I was not there, so I was not privy to the conversation. Perhaps there was a misunderstanding, but Jane interpreted it as a lack of welcome when Miss Bingley came to visit her a few days later. You would have to talk to your sister to discover more details." Lizzy neatly turned away from Bingley then, wanting him to have a chance to think about her words while she focused on Miss Georgiana. "How are you feeling, Miss Georgiana?"

The girl smiled. "I feel quite well, Miss Elizabeth. There was some recovery time after the incident, but a good rest at Pemberley worked wonders, and here I am in London for my first Season. You will be glad to know I did not trip while curtseying to Queen Charlotte at her ball."

Lizzy smiled. "I never feared you would. I have heard being presented at court is quite an experience." Her father, having little interest in London, had never made an effort to ensure she and her sisters curtsied before the queen. They had been introduced into Meryton society instead, which wasn't completely unconventional, but Lizzy felt like they had perhaps missed something with lacking a true first Season.

The rest of tea passed relatively pleasantly, though Darcy was a glowering presence of which Lizzy remained far more aware than she would like. Mr. Bingley shared the news he was hosting a ball at his townhouse that weekend and insisted the Bennet sisters must attend.

He magnanimously included their aunt and uncle as well, and Lizzy assured him she could see no reason why they wouldn't be there.

She managed to successfully avoid interaction with Darcy until it was time to depart, and he offered to walk her to the door. She hid a grimace of dismay, certain whatever he wanted to say would be nothing she wanted to hear. Most likely, he would attempt to dissuade her from accepting Mr. Bingley's invitation, though he must surely realize the futility of the undertaking.

She was endeavoring to leave as quickly as possible, though she still had to don her coat and hat, and as she buttoned the garment, he said, "You should stay away from Viscount Aumley."

She frowned, fingers stiffening and causing her to miss the buttonhole. That had been the last thing she expected him to say. "I beg your pardon?"

"The man is a rake."

She frowned at him, finding that difficult to believe. "What proof have you of that, Mr. Darcy?"

He opened his mouth to answer, and then he looked frustrated. "I am not... That is... It is simply an instinct. He is new to Society, and no one knows much about him. He could be a blackguard or a rake. A wise woman would be careful with her reputation."

"If your judgment is based purely on your own instinct and perceptions, pardon me for doubting the veracity of them, Mr. Darcy. After all, you have proven to be a poor judge of character. You still believe my dear sister is a fortune hunter, so I shall not be accepting your advice on the matter."

Before he could say anything else, she nodded to the butler, who'd observed the exchange with quiet disapproval, and he opened the door for her. She stepped out without words of parting to Darcy and started walking, soon leaving the grounds of Darcy House so she could flag down a hansom cab. She was irritated with his warning, and she put no stock in it. The man's perceptions couldn't be trusted when it came to judging people he considered inferior to him. He was always prone to think the worst.

Chapter Four

When Lizzy returned to Gracechurch Street, she found Jane in the sitting room. She sat down beside her, taking her sister's hands in hers and said, "I have the most wonderful news. I did not want to say anything earlier, because I was not certain it would lead anywhere, but I saw Mr. Bingley today when I had tea with Miss Georgiana Darcy."

Jane's eyes widened, and her hand trembled for a moment. "Indeed?" She seemed to be trying to sound uninterested, but her sparkling eyes gave her away. "Was he well?"

"Quite well, and quite unengaged to Miss Darcy, I assure you," said Lizzy with a gentle chuckle.

Jane's lips started to creep up into a smile. "That is welcome news."

"So is what I have to tell you. Mr. Bingley is having a rout this weekend at his townhouse, and he has invited us."

Jane let out an unladylike squeal of happiness before clamping a hand over her mouth after pulling it away from Lizzy's hand. She seemed to take a moment to compose herself, and she sounded far calmer when she spoke again. "That shall be a delightful event, I am certain."

"What shall be delightful?" asked Aunt Gardiner as she entered the room.

"We have been invited to a rout at Mr. Bingley's townhouse this weekend," said Lizzy in a meaningful fashion.

Her aunt's eyes widened, and the older woman clearly recognized the significance. No doubt, Jane had had a chance to confide in her during the time she had stayed there, and she looked pleased.

"I think an occasion like that calls for new gowns all around."

Lizzy shook her head. "We cannot accept that generosity, Aunt Gardiner."

"Indeed, you can," said Aunt Gardiner firmly. "I was just saying to your uncle not even yesterday that I needed a new gown, and I see no reason why you two should not have one as well."

Lizzy and Jane exchanged a glance, silently debating the matter before they both nodded. "If you insist, it would be rude to refuse," said Jane, though she sounded a little uncertain. "Are you certain, Aunt Gardiner?"

Her aunt nodded. "It is incumbent upon us to represent our house well, and I know for a fact none of us have dresses that are quite the caliber one needs for such illustrious society." She sounded like she was teasing them, since they all likely knew they had dresses that would work. They might be functional and slightly less ornate than the current style, but they would've been acceptable, nonetheless.

Lizzy recognized the gesture for what it was, and she reached out a hand to her aunt as Jane did the same. They squeezed Aunt Gardiner's hands simultaneously. Lizzy was smiling so much her face hurt. Surely, with a lovely new gown, and a softened demeanor now that Jane knew Caroline Bingley's hints about Charles and Georgiana were lies, it seemed inevitable the couple would reconcile.

"I was going to spend the afternoon reading, but I think we have a much more important pursuit. Let us go to the modiste, my dears." Aunt Gardiner got to her feet first, and Jane and Lizzy quickly complied. She followed her aunt and sister from the townhouse a few minutes later, and they took a hansom cab to the modiste's shop.

It was an engrossing hour as they looked at the current dress plates and fabrics, consulting with Mrs. Johnstone on what would be the most flattering for each. She took their measurements with the assistance of her shop girls and promised to have the dresses ready for a final fitting by Friday. Lizzy imagined her aunt was paying a little more for that privilege, and she winced at the thought, though she still appreciated the generosity.

After they had left the modiste's shop, Aunt Gardiner said, "Let us go by the tearoom and really indulge ourselves, my dears."

Jane gave an enthusiastic agreement, and Lizzy was about to confirm as well, but the boy hawking the newspaper caught her attention when he said, "Headless woman found."

She dropped Aunt Gardiner's arm to move closer to the boy, fetching a shilling from her reticule to hand him so she could buy a copy of the paper. He passed it over, and the front page bore the lurid headline about the headless woman. It also had a sketch of the person, who must've been identified through some means. Lizzy gasped and nearly dropped the paper when she recognized Marie Harris in the illustration.

Aunt Gardiner and Jane must have realized her distress, because they came over to join her. "Whatever is wrong?" asked Jane.

"You have gone dreadfully pale," said Aunt Gardiner.

Lizzy held out the paper to her aunt and sister. Aunt Gardiner winced at the headline, but Jane paled as well. "The assistant cook," said her sister.

Lizzy nodded. "She works for Mrs. Perkins, Aunt Gardiner. Perhaps we should call in to check on the household?" It seemed the thing to do, and Lizzy couldn't deny she wanted to know more about the circumstances. What kind of monster could do such a thing to such a sweet young woman?

Mrs. Gardiner looked troubled for a moment, and then she nodded. "Yes, I am certain Tilly would appreciate a call. This has no doubt been a shock for her and the entire household. We must defer tea, girls."

Neither Jane nor Lizzy offered a protest as they once more hailed a cab to take them to Mrs. Perkins's townhouse. When they arrived, there was a somber air about the place, and the butler showed them in with unrestrained dignity, but his eyes were red. Apparently, he was touched by the loss of his coworker as well.

Mrs. Perkins greeted them with a wail of distress, at first focusing on the tragic loss of young Marie, but then inevitably, her focus shifted to how the *ton* would perceive her since she was employing an assistant cook who had found herself in such a situation.

Lizzy had no patience for it, for she doubted very much Marie Harris had done anything to position herself as a victim, and she certainly hadn't designed to do so at the risk of exposing Mrs. Perkins to ridicule. Annoyed with the woman, she slipped away from the sitting room, certain no one noticed, and made her way back to the kitchen.

It was a more subdued staff she saw this time, and there was a large man she had not met the night she was there. She tapped at the doorway, hovering uncertainly as they all stared at her with ill-concealed shock for a moment before their postures straightened.

"How may we help you, miss?" asked the big man wearing the white apron. She assumed he was the chef Marie had mentioned before.

"I wanted to offer my condolences about Miss Harris. I had opportunity to meet her recently at a party your mistress hosted. She was quite a charming young woman."

The cook's expression softened, and he wiped at his face with the tail of his apron. "She was a lovely girl. Such promise, and her plum pudding was the most exquisite I had ever tasted."

Lizzy nodded as she moved closer, feeling slightly more confident in her welcome now. "I concur, sir. It was why we came to the kitchen, wanting to have a second helping."

The cook's eyes widened, and he clearly recognized the incident. "Miss Harris mentioned it to me the next morning with much pride. I am pleased you enjoyed what she produced."

Lizzy felt awkward standing there, but curiosity compelled her to ask, "Who would want to harm Miss Harris?"

There was a murmur among the staff, and the consensus was, "No one," said the cook firmly. "I cannot imagine how this happened, but it was certainly a case of mistaken identity or some other mishap. Miss Harris was a woman of impeccable morals."

As he said that, Lizzy saw one of the footmen who was polishing silver grimace, and she made a note of that. She quickly departed the kitchen after sharing her condolences again, waiting for the young man to emerge. She was hopeful he would come out first, and he did a short time later.

If he was startled to find her waiting for him, he didn't show it. It was almost as though he'd been looking for her, and there was an angry set to his expression. "She was not quite the paragon Mr. Beadles would have you believe."

Lizzy frowned. "Miss Harris?"

The man nodded. "Take my word for it."

"And who are you, sir?" asked Lizzy.

"I am Ollie. Until a few days ago, I was courting Marie. We were saving money so we could get married and leave service, but she broke up with me. She told me it was not going to work out, and that same night, I observed her slipping out of the house. She met a man in a black carriage."

Lizzy frowned. "Was this the night she was... Disappeared?"

He shook his head. "It was a couple of nights before that, but I would not be surprised if she sneaked out again to meet the same man. It was a fine coach, though I could not make out the details of the crest on the door, so she probably fell for some seducing rake above-stairs. Marie seemed like a sensible girl, but even a sensible girl can have her head turned by a charming scoundrel. I have no doubt she believed his sincerity, though the man was likely only dallying with her."

"Or worse," said Lizzy softly.

Ollie flinched then, apparently recognizing what her words implied. "You think the bloke who tried to seduce her might have been the one who hurt her?"

Lizzy hesitated. "I cannot profess to know much about the matters of the heart, but is it not plausible that someone denied what they wanted might fly into a rage?"

Ollie seemed to consider that, and it caused an odd reaction. He smiled slightly. "Perhaps she had not given away her virtue and given up all semblance of respect and decency then."

Lizzy considered that a unique way to see the bright side. Apparently, Ollie would prefer his once-intended to have died defending her honor rather than surrender it. She was disturbed by that, but she struggled not to show it as she excused herself and returned to the sitting room, pleased no one seemed to have noticed her absence.

Chapter Five

Thursday afternoon, Lizzy sat in the salon of an exclusive home in London, surrounded by people who were in general well above her rank. No one had been particularly unwelcoming, but she still felt out of place among them as she listened to Lord Aumley give his lecture on Kali.

It was obvious from the actions of the people around her that they gave little regard to the topic. They were busy whispering among themselves, and she didn't think they were discussing the contents of the lecture.

She found it quite rude, though she confessed his information wasn't nearly as compelling as she had thought it might be. For all his charm as a companion, he was a dreadful public speaker, who droned on and on and didn't interject any excitement into his voice. He managed to make human sacrifice sound as banal as taking tea with one's grandmother.

"The poor man is ghastly at this," said Tristan from beside her.

She turned and gave Mr. Nobles a small nod. "It is quite a juxtaposition to see how articulate he is in a personable way, yet he defaults to such a dry tone when delivering his academic lecture."

"It is all nonsense and babble anyway," said Tristan. "Who cares about the barbaric practices of followers of a heathen goddess, who demanded ritual sacrifice?"

"It is an upsetting topic," said Lizzy.

His lips twitched. "I do not find it the least upsetting. I find it all utterly pretentious though. These people pretend they are academics interested in other viewpoints and learning about the world, but they never step outside their own little place in it. They are happy to condemn the religious beliefs of an entire group of people, seeing it as further sign they are morally superior. It is all an affectation. Not one of them genuinely believes in any of this."

Lizzy's eyes widened at the passionate words, and she clutched her reticule tighter. "I suppose I cannot disagree with your assessment, but I find it comforting none of them believe in Kali. After all, we would hardly want someone making human sacrifices to the Indian goddess, would we?"

Tristan looked shocked by the idea, and then he shook his head. "No, that would be most appalling. Of course, I have no fear that Adam could do such a thing. The man could barely find it in himself to harm a fly, let alone a human, even if he does take this Kali nonsense a bit too seriously."

"I find that a reassuring bit of information. Not that I suspected anyone was about to begin ritual sacrifice in London," said Lizzy with a hint of amusement in her tone. The very notion was insane.

Or perhaps not quite so insane. Suddenly, she remembered Marie Harris in the state she'd been discovered. Lizzy quickly dismissed the idea it was an oblation to Kali. She had no explanation for what had happened to the poor girl yet, and she wasn't certain she could divine an answer, though she intended to search for one, but she was positive it had nothing to do with human sacrifice.

Chapter Six

Jane, Lizzy, and Aunt Gardiner retrieved their gowns on Friday. Only Lizzy's required a bit of adjustment in the bodice, for she felt it was too low to start with, and a fichu wouldn't provide enough coverage to suit her. After attaching a section of lace, it was more in line with her tastes, and the women collected their gowns and returned to the townhouse on Gracechurch Street to prepare for the evening ahead.

Jane was a vision in dusty rose when she joined them as they awaited the Gardiners' carriage. Uncle Gardiner didn't seem to have new evening attire for the occasion, but he also didn't appear to object to the three women having bought new gowns either. He praised each of them as lovely, and Lizzy couldn't deny she did feel quite beautiful in the violet gown with the lace at the bodice and intricate rosettes embroidered along the hems of the cap sleeves.

She wore gloves that went to midarm, and her hair was pinned and styled artfully by Aunt Gardiner's maid, with one curl curving down over her shoulder. She felt elegant, and she was confident when she emerged from the carriage in front of the townhouse at Grosvenor Street. She girded herself for battle, fully expecting a scene with Caroline Bingley, though it might not be an overt one.

She maintained her confidence when they entered the townhouse, and the butler announced their arrival. It was a far more elegant rout than Lizzy had ever attended, since most of hers had been confined to social gatherings hosted by families in and around Meryton, along with an occasional outing in London.

She couldn't help craning her head to look around, feeling a bit like a wide-eyed ingénue in her first Season, and realizing that wasn't too far off the mark. These were the kinds of events other women in her station and above would have had in their first Season and would've already taken for granted by the time they reached the age of twenty like Lizzy.

Mr. Bingley greeted them as soon as they stepped off the stairs, immediately approaching Jane. He took her hand in his and brought it to his lips. "It is lovely to see you again, Miss Bennet."

"I am so happy to see you as well, Mr. Bingley. There is much I would like to discuss with you." Jane appeared to be maintaining her courage well. Lizzy approved that her sister planned to fully tackle the subject head-on and explain why she had been so cool at the Netherfield ball. It seemed like the best way to clear the air between them.

"Perhaps we could talk while we dance?" asked Mr. Bingley.

Jane hesitated and then nodded. "Perhaps so."

"May I request your next two dances?"

Jane had just given her agreement when Caroline approached, looking as though she'd been sucking on a lemon. She frowned at Jane. "I did not expect to see you here, Miss Bennet."

Jane's expression tightened, and she was the closest thing to angry that Lizzy had seen. "No doubt, you did not expect that, Miss Bingley, but Mr. Bingley invited me through Lizzy, and it would be rude to refuse." Her tone was cold, and Lizzy was proud of her sister for making her displeasure known. She had been afraid Jane would try to make amends when she had done nothing wrong.

Caroline seemed shocked by her tone, but she had no chance to reply as the music changed, indicating the next set was about to begin, and Mr. Bingley took Jane's arm to lead her to the dance floor. He didn't spare a glance or a word for his sister. Indeed, he seemed unable to look at anyone or anything but Jane.

Caroline turned to glare at Lizzy, as though this were her fault. "I am certainly surprised to see you here."

"Mr. Bingley invited us when I had tea with Miss Darcy the other day."

Caroline looked upset then. "Miss Georgiana invited you for tea?"

Lizzy smiled, trying not to be too unkind. She didn't want Caroline to suffer too much, though the woman probably deserved every ounce of it. "We did become quite good friends during our brief time at Netherfield. We happened to run into each other at the museum the other day when she was with Fitzwilliam...Mr. Darcy, and she invited me for tea."

Lizzy had deliberately used Fitzwilliam's first name, hoping to provoke Caroline. It worked, as the other woman's pale complexion took on a flushed tinge, and her eyes sparkled with obvious anger. Before she could say anything more, Lizzy's attention shifted to a man approaching. She gave him a genuine smile of pleasure as Adam came to stand beside her. "Ah, Lord Aumley, I did not know you would be here."

"Mr. Bingley and I have some interactions upon occasion. We are in a similar line of business."

"How lovely." She turned deliberately from Caroline, who was still clearly caught in the throes of outrage. "My dance card remains dreadfully unfilled at the moment, Lord Aumley," she said in a leading fashion.

He frowned. "That simply will not do. You must allow me to reserve the next two."

Lizzy smiled at him. "I would be delighted." Before they went to dance, she ensured Uncle Gardiner had been properly introduced to Adam, and then he whisked her onto the floor when the music started for the next set.

"Miss Bingley looked ready to combust." He sounded vaguely amused.

"She had something unexpected occur. It must have upset her greatly."

"Were you the architect of her suffering?"

Lizzy shook her head as she made the next dance step, pressing her palm to his for a moment as the formation dictated. "No, it was truly a bit of accident all around. If you had not invited me to the British Museum, it would not have set the possibility in motion."

His eyes gleamed. "So, I am the architect of her suffering?"

Lizzy shrugged a shoulder. "You or fate. I suppose it depends on who would wish to take credit."

He looked uneasy. "I confess, Miss Bingley intimidates me, and she seems to have little use for me the few times we have interacted, but I would not wish to make her upset. She must be too gently bred to deliberately injure."

Lizzy couldn't help thinking he simply didn't know her well enough yet, but she patted his arm in a commiserating fashion as she moved past him. "That is most humble of you, Lord Aumley. You can hardly be blamed for the situation, and truly, it is nothing that should pain her. It does not directly affect her, and instead, it might ensure the happiness of two people." Her gaze moved to Charles and Jane, who were farther down the formation.

His gaze followed, and he seemed to intuit at least part of the situation, though he had no knowledge of the background. "In that case, I cannot regret my part in the situation. Indeed, I cannot regret inviting you anyway, for spending time with you is intoxicating, Miss Bennet."

Alerted by the smoky turn of his voice, she was afraid he was starting to form more than friendship for her. She averted her gaze quickly, unexpectedly locking eyes with Darcy, who stood at the corner of the dance floor. It was hardly surprising he wasn't dancing, but his cold expression and clear anger bore down upon her even across the distance separating them.

Hastily, she looked away, her gaze once more clashing with Adam's. It was full of earnest hope, and she felt a sinking sensation in her chest. As much as she wanted to like Adam, she was certain she never could in that way. All it had taken was one angry glance shared with Fitzwilliam Darcy to recall just how he made her feel.

He enraged her to no end, and he was as prideful and prejudicial as he'd ever been, and far too prone to meddling with other people's emotions and relationships, but Lizzy couldn't deny she was drawn to him. It could never work, for how could she love a man who considered her inferior, and who blatantly regarded her sister as a fortune seeker? Still, how she felt about Darcy was enough to underscore how she didn't feel about Adam and was certain she never would.

When the dance ended, she stepped back. "Perhaps we could get some fresh air instead of a second dance for now, Lord Aumley?"

He nodded, appearing eager to assist her. "You do look flushed."

No doubt she was, having had the unexpected epiphany right in the middle of the dance floor. She strove to collect her composure as she followed him close to the balcony. They did not step out, but the door was open and allowed a cool breeze to come in, which took some of the heat from her face. Adam thoughtfully hovered nearby, and Lizzy searched for a way to make it clear she wasn't interested in him in a romantic way.

"Do you remember Miss Darcy from the museum?" Her gaze sought out the young woman in the crowd.

"I do, though I have not had a chance to speak with her beyond that limited exchange. This is her first Season, is it not?"

She nodded. "She is on the shy side, and I have no doubt it would be a confidence boost to her if you would seek her out to request a dance or two."

Adam frowned slightly. "You wish for me to dance with another woman?"

She smiled at him. "I could hardly expect you to content yourself with just two dances, and we all know propriety dictates that is all I can allot you. I do believe you would have quite a bit in common with Miss Darcy. She is a sweet young woman, though she does not seem to prefer the museum."

He smiled, though he still looked vaguely troubled. "I would much prefer to spend my time with a woman who appreciates history."

"It is never a good idea to tie yourself to one friend, Lord Aumley. You are likely to end up disappointed if that friend does not give you everything you want. I always find it advisable to maintain a wider circle of acquaintances." Lizzy admired how confident she sounded and sure of the knowledge she was imparting. It was a complete ruse, but she hoped it was subtle enough to convey the message she wanted to send—she would be unable to give Adam what he seemed to want from her.

He looked crestfallen for a moment, but then he rallied. "If you are up to being left alone, I shall seek out Miss Darcy. I will claim my second dance later, if that is acceptable?"

"Of course." She smiled at him. "I do find myself feeling much better. You can safely leave me."

"As you wish, Miss Bennet." He returned to the ballroom, soon seeking out Georgiana.

Lizzy had barely stepped back into the room when Tristan was there, asking, "May I have this dance, Miss Bennet?"

She nodded at him as she accepted his arm before she curtsied to him, as was part of the start of the dance, and they began moving together. He was eyeing her with admiration, and she wondered if she was going to have a similar problem with him.

Fortunately, his words were not at all flirtatious when he said, "You remind me of my mother, Miss Bennet."

Her eyes widened. "I do?"

He nodded. "I lost her when I was young, only eleven, but she was so graceful. There were many times I would sneak to the top of the stairs and watch her and Papa entertain, and she always danced with such lively elegance."

Lizzy flushed with the compliment. "I would hardly call myself graceful, but I thank you. I will certainly not argue if you see a resemblance between your mother and myself. I find that most flattering."

"She was indeed a special woman." He cleared his throat after a moment. "Now, for less maudlin talk, how was your trip to Mr. Bingley's home?"

"The ride was without remarkability. And you?"

He grinned. "My townhouse is nearby, so it was a brief walk for me. Most invigorating, though I did consider taking a sedan chair to save my shoes."

"The weather has been fine for this time of year," said Lizzy. "We have not seen much snow yet."

"I fear that will change soon, having seen the gray clouds and a little bit of pink in the sky earlier."

Lizzy nodded, having made the same observation. "It will be nice to have some snow again, but not too much."

They passed the rest of the dance discussing mundane topics, and he did not request a second one. Lizzy returned to her aunt and uncle, who were busy speaking with people she didn't know, but they clearly recognized. After sharing introductions, she contributed here and there, spending the next few dances in conversation when no one had asked her to accompany them to the dance floor.

Lizzy was fine with that. After having reached the unwelcome realization she cared more about Darcy than she wanted to, she was in no state of mind to handle meaningless flirtation or try to sort out the motives of men who might want to dance with her. Was it benign and a bit of fun, or did they have something more serious in mind? It was all exhausting to think about.

She was dismayed when Mr. Darcy escorted Caroline onto the dancefloor a few moments later. There was nothing improper in how they faced each other, but she still resented how close Caroline was to Darcy, and how she looked up at him with clear adoration. Determined to ignore the spectacle, and her reaction to it, she deliberately turned away.

She had been pleased to see Miss Georgiana dancing with the viscount two dances in a row, and shortly after that, Georgiana found her by the punch bowl. She poured herself a cup of ratafia, and Lizzy refilled her own.

"The viscount hinted you might have suggested he ask me to dance," said Georgiana, her eyes sparkling. "I thank you for the attention, dear friend." She smiled. "He is a charming fellow, is he not?"

Lizzy nodded. "He is, though I fear you might have some interests that might not converge with his. He is quite engrossed in history and religion."

Georgiana grimaced slightly. "And he does not know much about music, yet he is still a charming companion."

Before Lizzy could respond, Darcy approached then, standing near them. He was giving his sister an indulgent smile, though it melted from his face when he looked at Lizzy. His words were shocking when he said, "I would like to request a dance with you, Miss Bennet."

She was on the verge of refusing, but how could she do so? If she did, it would consign her to being unable to dance with anyone else for the rest of the evening, and Georgiana would question why she was refusing to dance with her brother. She suspected he had timed it thusly on purpose, and she gritted her teeth as she nodded. "I would be pleased," she said in a tone that lacked any conviction.

If Georgiana noticed her lack of enthusiasm, she didn't say anything as she gestured for them to go on to the dance floor, assuring her brother she would be fine. Darcy had clearly realized her lack of willingness though, because he was stiff beside her as he took her arm to lead her to the dance floor.

They hovered for a few minutes, waiting for the current set to end, and she half-expected him to say something to irritate her, but he must've decided to maintain his silence. She truly couldn't divine his strategy for dancing with her, but it soon became obvious when they fell into step together, and they were facing each other. "I see you chose not to heed my warning about Aumley."

"Adam is a nice young man, and you have misjudged him. Your sister thinks he is nice as well."

His lips tightened. "I want you to stay away from him. You cannot trust him."

She rolled her eyes. "Because you say so?"

He nodded firmly and seemed utterly convinced.

Lizzy shook her head slightly. "As you know my opinion on your ability to judge others, I shall not be lending it much weight. In fact, one could accuse you of being jealous." As she uttered the accusation, she expected him to rebuff it decisively.

Instead, he stared at her for a long moment, his face serious. "I am, but I still have a bad feeling about the young man. We know nothing about him, and I do not wish to see you risk your reputation."

Her eyes widened at his admission, and she stumbled to a halt. Darcy kept her from falling, and they stared at each other for a long moment. It was only when she heard someone clear their throat behind them that she realized they were holding up the dance procession, and she started moving again.

"You admit to being jealous?" She tried to phrase it academically, but there was the slightest bit of pleasure bleeding through her tone. It was a ridiculous reaction, for she should be dismayed that he still had any sort of emotion for her, not pleased about it.

"I admit to it," he said in a starched tone.

"I admit to some jealousy seeing you with Caroline Bingley," said Lizzy with unanticipated honesty. She hadn't planned to reveal that to him, but now that the words were out, she couldn't bring herself to regret uttering them.

His gaze locked on hers again, and though they managed to keep moving, it felt like her entire world was at a standstill. "I find that information interesting," he said in an almost bland tone. "It is a wonder you so firmly rejected my offer if you feel such a way."

Lizzy couldn't deny feeling a hint of regret at having to do so, but she kept her tone gentle when she said, "You insulted me with your proposal, Mr. Darcy, which I could forgive. If I had given serious thought to entertaining the idea, I could have overcome your phrasing. After all, you said nothing but what you perceive as the truth, and there is a great deal of truth to what you said."

"Yet you still refused me." He sounded as though the matter was a topic of general conversation and nothing important to him.

She nodded. As he spun her around, she saw Jane and Charles and pointed to them discreetly. "Have you revised your opinion of Jane?"

He hesitated for a moment, but then he shook his head. He seemed reluctant to be honest, but he didn't have it in him to lie. "I have not. I still think she is a lovely young woman, but I do not see that she has any real regard for Charles."

Lizzy couldn't imagine how he could be so blind. Her sister was smiling up at Charles with such an open expression, and her eyes gleamed with pleasure. Mr. Darcy must be willfully blinding himself to the proof of her sister's affection, so he didn't have to question his judgment.

"That is why I could never say yes to you, Mr. Darcy. You go out of your way to deliberately thwart Jane's happiness, and you refuse to reconsider." To her relief, the music ended then, and she took a step back. "Thank you for the dance."

When she turned around, Adam was waiting for her, clearly intent on claiming his second dance. She accepted it as she fell into line with him, and he soon invited her to go on a ride through Hyde Park at four o'clock the next afternoon. Lizzy agreed, catching Tristan's eye over Adam's shoulder. His friend was smiling benevolently at them, and she was afraid he might be a matchmaking sort too. Perhaps while she was out riding with Adam tomorrow, she would have another opportunity to make it clear she wanted only friendship with the young viscount.

Chapter Seven

Fitzwilliam clenched his hands into fists as he shamelessly eavesdropped on Lizzy's conversation with Lord Aumley. She was planning to ride with him tomorrow in the park, and he had a hard time controlling his rage. She could flirt so carelessly with a man whom Fitzwilliam distrusted, but she could ignore how she felt for him? He did not understand her at all, but that was generally the way of it. Women were often complex and perplexing, and Lizzy Bennet was no exception.

With a sigh, he started to turn away, but Caroline Bingley's hand fell on his shoulder then, and he stiffened slightly as he turned to look at her. "How are you this evening, Miss Caroline?" He had danced with her previously, having managed to escape after just one dance, and there had been little opportunity for conversation, since it had been one of the livelier quadrilles. He had timed it perfectly when he asked her to dance, hoping to share such an enthusiastic dance with her to minimize both conversation opportunities and girlish fantasies on her part. It was clear she was here for a second one, and if he walked away, it would be incomparably rude, especially since her brother was the host. "Would you like to dance again?"

She smiled, her lips softening, and she had a dewy glow about her complexion. She was indeed a lovely woman, but he could feel nothing for her as she accepted his invitation, and he swept her onto the dance floor. It was a slower song, and the configuration allowed for more face-to-face interaction, so they were able to converse more.

She chatted on about inconsequential things to start with, but then her voice lowered. "I have done everything I can to keep the Bennet woman away from my brother, but I am at a loss. What would you suggest we do next, Mr. Darcy?"

The note of intimacy in her tone worried him, and he realized Caroline thought they were conspiring against the situation together. She likely took it as encouragement that he was prepared to work with her again on other matters, and that would lead her to expect something more from him.

He had never had interest in marrying Caroline Bingley, and that hadn't changed. Even if he hadn't met Lizzy Bennet and lost his heart, he was certain he never could've accepted Caroline. He kept his voice gentle when he said, "I think we have done all we can, Miss Bingley. The rest is up to Charles now. If he cannot see the truth, we can do nothing to save him."

She frowned. "I cannot tolerate that. You should come to tea tomorrow afternoon, and we shall form a plan together."

He shook his head. "Regretfully, I am committed to other activities tomorrow afternoon. I do not believe it is wise to continue meddling. We have tried to save Charles, but ultimately, it is Charles's decision, and we risk our relationships with him if we persist."

Caroline clearly disliked his words. "You are saying I should just meekly accept that woman into the family? You have seen her relations. Her family has no breeding. For goodness sake, Miss Eliza is perhaps the second best of the lot, and you know how low she is."

"Miss Elizabeth has impeccable manners," said Darcy stiffly.

Caroline's eyes narrowed. "That is quite a contrary opinion from what you used to have, Mr. Darcy." Her tone was tart.

He shrugged a shoulder. "Perhaps I have reconsidered my stance."

She seemed genuinely shocked. "You never change your estimation, Mr. Darcy. Once someone has lost your good opinion, it is lost forever."

He looked at her repressively. "Perhaps I am attempting to change, Miss Bingley. Maybe I have been wrong about certain assumptions."

She appeared frozen in shock for a moment, and she missed a step. He carried her through it, and she seemed impatient for the dance to end then. He wondered if he had finally found a way to ward off Caroline Bingley's interest.

Deciding he might have, he said, "I have come to know Miss Elizabeth better, and I admire a lot about her. Perhaps she is correct in her assessment that Miss Jane loves Bingley. I suggest we should both reevaluate our opinions and try to keep an open mind, Miss Bingley."

She glared at him, and it was obvious from her body language she was rejecting the thought without any serious consideration. "Indeed, what a turnabout from you." She sounded somewhere between angry and betrayed as she stepped back from him when the music ended. He bowed to her, but she didn't bother with the cursory curtsey as expected when she turned on her heel and stormed away. He couldn't regret having alienated her, because it finally seemed like she might be accepting he would never marry her.

HAVING OVERHEARD HER plans to ride with Aumley the next afternoon, Darcy took Goliath for a ride at the opportune time, soon picking out Elizabeth's glossy head of hair ahead of him. She sat on a phaeton beside Aumley, who wore his top hat, but Lizzy's bonnet was pushed back in a haphazard fashion, and he found it charming rather than irritating that she wasn't a stickler for wearing it this time of day.

Likely, she was appreciating the sunlight beaming down on them, and since it was a rare sunny afternoon in the insipid gray of a typical London January day, he could appreciate it himself. Impulsively, he removed his top hat in solidarity, ignoring the wide eyes of the two women beside him in their own phaeton. He nodded to them in a respectful fashion and urged Goliath forward.

He wanted to be nearer to observe Lizzy's interactions with the viscount should he need to intercede. Once he got close enough to overhear their conversation while maintaining discretion, he was surprised to find their topics of conversation were almost mind-numbingly mundane.

His attention wavered when he heard a cry. He turned in that direction, though it was difficult to make any progress with the crush of fashionables on the promenade, as he heard someone shout out, "There is a body in the pond."

He should have been surprised, but he wasn't when he saw Lizzy scrambling down from Aumley's phaeton, ignoring his cries for her to return as she plunged through the crowd, heading in the direction of the cry about the body. Darcy was glad he had brought Goliath rather than a carriage, because that gave him slightly more maneuverability, and though the horse was slowed more than Lizzy was, he arrived shortly after her.

Someone had already pulled the body from the water, and he noticed immediately the woman's head was missing. It was a distressing sight, and he rushed to Lizzy. Before he could think better of it, he took her into his arms and pressed her face against his chest. "You should not look."

To his surprise, she melted against him, clutching his back as she nodded. "Yes." The word was more of a whimper than a sound.

He looked around, deciding the most expedient way out of the crush was on Goliath's back. He pulled on the reins, and the horse came closer so he could put Lizzy on the saddle, seating her sideways to maintain some of her dignity before mounting behind her. He spurred Goliath gently, and they were soon away from Hyde Park.

He stopped at the first tearoom he saw, dismounting the horse before wrapping the reins around the hitching post and returning to Lizzy to lift her down. "Let us get some tea to fortify ourselves."

Lizzy was more composed than he had expected, though she was still clearly upset, because her hand trembled when she took a cup of tea a few minutes later. Since she was distracted, he poured a generous dollop of cream and extra sugar in it, thinking she needed the fortification. She sipped it in appreciation and nodded, though she still looked haunted. "I had to see for myself, I guess. It immediately made me think of Marie."

Fitzwilliam was in the process of liberally sugaring his own tea, but he paused to look at her. "Who is Mary?"

"*Marie* Harris. She was a lovely young woman." Lizzy quickly apprised him of the situation, and the poor girl's ultimate fate.

He frowned as he finished stirring his tea. "She was found in a similar fashion?"

Lizzy nodded, looking distraught. "Who would do such a thing? And to two women?"

"They might not be related."

Lizzy bit her lip. "I suppose that is possible, but it is such a lurid way to kill someone, so it seems unlikely someone would lose himself in the heat of the moment and decapitate someone, let alone twice in a week. I think they must be related somehow."

Darcy couldn't argue with her, though he had hoped to soothe her. It did seem an astonishing coincidence that two women could be murdered in such a fashion and not have the same murderer. "You said the young man witnessed Miss Harris getting into a black carriage?"

Lizzy nodded. "He could not make out the crest though."

Darcy frowned. "Lord Aumley has a black carriage."

Lizzy's eyes widened, and then she looked at him with her lips pursed. "Tell me, Mr. Darcy, what color is your carriage?"

He reared back slightly, parting grudgingly with the answer. "Black."

"Indeed? What a coincidence. I count most of the carriages I saw today must have been black."

"And your point?" Even as he asked, he knew.

"Black is a common color, and you have an admitted grudge against the viscount. Just because he has a black carriage does not make him a murderer, and I was with him this afternoon when we discovered the body."

"True, but I doubt the young woman had been placed there in just the last few minutes."

Lizzy shrugged. "Who knows? Surely, that is the sort of thing someone would have noticed quickly, so it could have been arranged just before the height of popularity for riding through Hyde Park to see and be seen."

He had to concede that as well. "You were with him an hour ago?"

She started to nod and then hesitated. "Perhaps not an hour ago. He fetched me from Aunt and Uncle Gardiner's home, and then we made the ride to the park. I suppose it would have been possible for him to place the body in the pond before he picked me up. I am not saying it is likely though," she swiftly added.

He felt benevolent now that she had conceded his point. "But possible. You should steer clear of the man."

"I shall be cautious, but I am hardly likely to condemn him to a lack of interaction simply because of one possibility, and the coincidence of him having a black carriage like half of London."

He glowered at her, knowing he had little hope of persuading her without more proof. His jealousy and unease weren't enough to convince her, and when viewed logically, he could see why. He was in no mood to look at it rationally though. He simply wanted to ensure Lizzy stopped associating with the man, but he couldn't figure out a way to make that happen yet.

Instead, he said, "I suggest we speak with a Runner tomorrow. They are sure to have more information by then, and you can share what you know as well. With me along to escort you, there will be no impropriety about you going to Bow Street."

Her eyes widened for a moment, and then she nodded slowly. "I must admit, we do make a fair team when it comes to solving these sorts of situations. Yes, that is a good suggestion, and I believe it would be wise to get the expertise of a Runner. For though we have tackled abduction, theft, and extortion, murder is new for both of us." Despite the grisly discovery of the last hour, she was looking better now, and there was a hint of color in her cheeks.

He found it most charming, and he wished he could always see her like this, smiling across the table from him, though of course, her smile was tempered by the horror of what they had seen, and by the seriousness of the possible murder of two women. His enthusiasm was also lacking for the task at hand, though he could think of no one else with whom he would rather work on this matter than Lizzy Bennet.

Chapter Eight

Lizzy wasn't certain how she felt about working with Darcy again, though she was glad to have a partner. She knew he was competent and would be a good assistant, but she worried the conflict simmering between them might impede the investigation. Despite her reservations, she was waiting when his carriage pulled up outside Gracechurch Street the next morning, hurrying out to meet him so they could keep to their schedule.

His driver opened the door for her, and she slipped into the carriage with him, taking the seat across from Darcy while unable not to observe how handsome he was this morning. There was nothing particularly different about him, but she was noticing it more prevalently. She shook her head, attempting to dismiss the thoughts, as she greeted him politely. He returned the greeting, and they endured mainly in silence as the carriage ferried them from her aunt and uncle's house to Bow Street.

It stopped several minutes later, and the door opened seconds after that. Darcy departed first, and he held out a hand to assist her. Lizzy took it, trying not to tremble when their fingers touched, though layers of gloves separated them. He quickly released her hand as soon as she was on her feet on the ground, but he offered his arm, and she took it. She hated how being in his proximity left her discombobulated.

Vowing to focus her attention on the matter at hand, she straightened her shoulders and entered the office with him. It was a busy little building, filled with men shouting to each other while clerks bustled about. There were a few other people waiting who appeared in need of a Runner's service, but Darcy ignored them as he went to the front desk, telling the young man stationed there, "I have an appointment with Joseph Kenton this morning. My name is Fitzwilliam Darcy."

The young man looked at the appointment book before nodding and coming around the desk to personally show them to Mr. Kenton's desk. Lizzy took the only seat positioned in front of it, eyeing the Runner with whom Darcy had made the appointment.

He was a young man, probably no more than five or six years older than Kitty, with dark skin, closely cropped curls, and big brown eyes that revealed intelligence and inquisitiveness. She instantly felt at ease around him, certain he was competent.

He nodded to both of them before gesturing for one of his coworkers to slide over a chair for Mr. Darcy. When they were both seated in front of his desk, he said, "I received your missive, Mr. Darcy. You wanted to discuss a murder?"

"Two murders," said Lizzy. "We suspect they might be linked."

His brows drew together as he leaned back slightly. "Go on, Miss...?"

"Elizabeth Bennet," she said crisply. Then she spent the next few minutes telling him about the two murdered women, and how they suspected there might be a link.

He looked grey when she had finished, and he rose higher in her estimation when he didn't look at Mr. Darcy for confirmation of her words. "I do have that file on my desk, assuming it might be what Mr. Darcy referenced. I am referring to the young woman found in the park yesterday. Her name was Katherine Mansfield, and she worked as a modiste's assistant."

He reached for a file and opened it, shuffling through pages until he found what he was looking for. A moment later, he placed the drawing in front of Lizzy and Darcy, and she realized it was a rendering of Katherine Mansfield. She resembled Marie strongly, and Lizzy felt a prickle of unease, though she couldn't determine why until Mr. Darcy spoke.

"She could be your sister," he said, looking troubled.

Lizzy looked closer, realizing he was right. There was a striking resemblance between her and Katherine, and she recalled Marie's image in her mind, realizing she also bore the same dark hair, dark eyes, and heart-shaped face. "Marie Harris also shared the same features."

Joseph Kenton stood up. "Give me a moment. I believe we have that file as well." He walked across the room to confer with another young man, and after a few seconds of exchange, he returned with a file he placed on his desk before sitting down. He opened it with methodical precision and found the illustration of Marie. He placed it beside Katherine's, and the resemblance was uncanny. Lizzy couldn't deny the three of them shared a similar look.

"You could be at risk, Lizzy," said Darcy.

She stiffened her shoulders and shook her head in automatic rejection. "Why would I be at risk? It is unlikely I have even met the murderer."

"Yet you are tangentially connected to both women, having met Miss Harris before her death, and having been one of the first to find Miss Mansfield's body," said Mr. Kenton. "Is there someone who might target you?"

"Lord Aumley," said Darcy harshly.

Lizzy barely resisted the urge to roll her eyes. "The viscount has been nothing but polite. You have no reason to suspect him other than personal ones, Mr. Darcy."

"Nonetheless, it would be wise to watch out for your safety at this time, Miss Bennet. It is better to proceed with an abundance of caution than to act recklessly." Mr. Kenton made a notation on a piece of paper on his desk. "Miss Mansfield's murder is my top priority, and I shall apprise you of updates as permitted."

They took their leave a short time later, and Darcy still seemed troubled as he handed her into the carriage, not leaving the task to his driver. He followed her, and brooding silence hung between them. Lizzy tapped her fingers impatiently on her knee, wishing to return to Gracechurch Street and forget about the startling resemblance she bore to the two victims.

"I believe we can concur they were killed by the same man," said Darcy.

Lizzy nodded, having assumed that all along. "What persuaded you?"

"He appears to have a type. I have already agreed it was quite an astronomical coincidence to have two such murders carried out in the same fashion occur in the same month, but having recognized another link between his victims, I am certain this man is targeting women of your appearance."

Her lips tightened. "That does not mean I am at risk, Mr. Darcy."

"Nor does it mean you are safe. It is wise to have someone with you at all times until the man is apprehended."

"It could be a woman, you know."

His eyes widened. "What?"

"The murderer could be a woman."

Darcy irritated her by laughing. "What woman would have the ability to commit such atrocities with cold calculation?"

Lizzy hesitated and then shrugged. "I do not know of one necessarily, but I feel you are impeding our investigation by automatically dismissing half the population as possible suspects."

His mouth tightened. "There is no investigation, Miss Bennet. If the killer has a type, you certainly conform to it, and there is no reason to bring yourself into his sphere of notice. We should leave the matter to Mr. Kenton."

Lizzy thought about arguing, but she didn't have a compelling way to persuade him. After all, how would she investigate? Being able to talk to Ollie and discovering his information had been more a stroke of luck than skill, and she didn't have a similar opening with Miss Mansfield, since she had never met the woman.

She could hardly go poking around into her life trying to find a connection, and Mr. Kenton would be far more successful with the reputation and respect of the Bow Street Runners behind him. Despite her skill at piecing together mysteries, she was out of her depths with this one.

When they drew up outside Gracechurch Street a few minutes later, the driver opened the door, and Lizzy stepped down. She turned to issue a parting to Mr. Darcy before realizing he was accompanying her.

She frowned at him, but she could hardly refuse to allow him entry. It would be unspeakably rude, so she led him up the walk and into the house moments later. Aunt Gardiner came to meet them, and Mr. Darcy greeted her warmly, almost as if they were old friends. After a few moments of polite conversation, he said, "I would like to speak with Mr. Gardiner. Is he available?"

Aunt Gardiner nodded and pointed to Uncle Gardiner's study. "He decided to work from home today. He has a fine view of his factory from that window and often avails himself of his home office to escape the noise."

With a nod for both, Darcy crossed the room. Lizzy, compelled by curiosity and a hint of unease, followed him, but he closed the door in her face. She stared at it aghast for a moment before anger took over. She briefly considered opening the door and entering anyway, but her outrage increased when she heard the lock click a second later, as though he had read her mind. Surely, she wasn't that predictable?

With a huff, she flounced across the room and threw herself onto the settee as Aunt Gardiner took a wingback, looking concerned. "Do you know what they are discussing?" asked her aunt.

Lizzy shrugged a shoulder. "I have no idea, but I do have suspicions."

Her aunt's eyes widened, and she seemed on the verge of smiling. "What fabulous news. This is indeed a reason to celebrate. Fanny will be beside herself with joy."

Lizzy, whose mind was still focused on the investigation, couldn't follow her aunt's leap in logic. "I beg your pardon?"

"He is here to ask for permission to court you, is he not? Or is he here to request your hand already?" Her aunt's eyes gleamed with excitement. "That would be a splendid thing indeed. The Darcy family is a fine bunch, and I know some about them from having grown up in Lambton. They were always a good family and good to the people in the community."

Lizzy put up a hand before her aunt, who wasn't generally prone to excitement or false conclusions, could throw herself into planning a wedding that would never occur. "Aunt Gardiner, please slow down. I can assure you Darcy is not speaking to my uncle about courting me or marrying me. Beyond that, I am not entirely certain his purpose for speaking with him. Even if it were the topic Mr. Darcy wanted to introduce, I could never accept him as a husband."

Her aunt frowned. "Why ever not? There is clearly attraction between you."

Lizzy gasped at her aunt's words, and her face flushed with heat. She snapped open her fan and waved it furiously. "I do not know where you have gotten such an impression."

Her aunt gave her a direct look. "You are old enough to discuss certain realities, Lizzy, and it is obvious to anyone with eyes when you two interact there is something more than friendship there."

Lizzy shook her head. "I submit you are incorrect, Aunt Gardiner. Besides, even if I had affection for Mr. Darcy, I could never accept his offer of marriage. He is deliberately thwarting Jane's attempts to be with Mr. Bingley because he considers her unworthy. He claims she has no true regard for his friend."

Her aunt sniffed. "What nonsense. The girl lights up in his presence. Yet, I suppose I could see how Mr. Darcy reached that conclusion. Jane is a rather quiet and reserved girl, tending to keep her emotions to herself, especially in public settings and with people she does not know. That might come across as aloof rather than shy."

Lizzy's mouth dropped open. "Are you defending his actions?"

"No. I am simply pointing out I see how he might have reached that conclusion. There must be a way to persuade him to change his mind."

Lizzy snorted. "I wish you luck with that, dear aunt, for the man's impressions and opinions are intractable. Indeed, they might as well be set in stone."

Her aunt frowned. "There must be a way to ensure your sister has happiness so you might as well."

"My happiness would not be with Mr. Darcy, I assure you," said Lizzy tartly. She was relieved the topic of conversation had to be set aside when her uncle's study door opened that moment, and the two men emerged. Right away, she could see her uncle was concerned by the set of his shoulders and his dark expression.

He came over and sat beside her, leaving Mr. Darcy to take another wingback. Uncle Gardiner took her hand in his, saying, "Mr. Darcy has explained the situation."

"What situation?" asked Aunt Gardiner, looking alarmed.

Lizzy didn't bother to answer. She just glared at Darcy, while imagining what he might've told her uncle. "He is assuming there is a risk that might not exist. There is no proof anyone has targeted me."

Her aunt started fanning herself. "Targeted you? For what? What is going on, Edward?"

Her uncle looked up. "I shall explain it all to you in a moment, Madeline." Then he returned his attention to Lizzy. "Mr. Darcy has suggested, and I agree, that you should not go out unaccompanied.

Until the matter is resolved, and the culprit is apprehended, you are to stay here in the townhouse unless I can accompany you somewhere. Mr. Darcy has also offered his assistance."

Lizzy's mouth dropped open wider, and she glared at Darcy. "I will be a prisoner here for no reason?"

Her uncle made a scoffing sound. "You are hardly to be a prisoner. You simply must have an escort."

She looked at her uncle. "You will be happy to take me to the museum, or the lending library, or the tearoom?"

Her uncle looked dismayed at the possibility. "I do have to work many hours per day, my dear."

"So, I am indeed a prisoner. Does Aunt Gardiner count as a permissible guardian?"

Her uncle frowned, seeming to consider the matter. "I hesitate to disappoint you, but I fear Madeline might not be adequate. If you are physically at risk, your aunt would be unable to provide assistance."

With each word, Aunt Gardiner looked more and more concerned, and Lizzy sighed. "Perhaps you should speak with my aunt and explain it all to her."

Uncle nodded and stood up, taking Aunt Gardiner by the hand and leading her from the room to his study.

Lizzy was glad to have a moment alone with Darcy. "I hope you are happy. No doubt, you had some scheme in mind for setting this in motion. Do you imagine having me confined here will keep my sister from being able to interact with Mr. Bingley?"

His expression darkened, and his face tightened, but he sounded relatively mild when he said, "If you desire entertainment, we are having a ball at Darcy House this weekend. You and your sister must attend, and I will escort you myself."

Lizzy wanted to refuse, wishing to toss back the offer in his face in a dramatic gesture, but she realized how happy Jane would be at another chance to see Mr. Bingley. By the weekend, she would probably be sick of staring at the four walls around her and eager to escape her confinement to the townhouse. "Very well, Mr. Darcy. We shall be your guests." She spoke as though she were granting him a favor, and his lips twitched in response, though he had the good sense not to laugh.

"How very sensible of you, Miss Bennet."

"I still resent your interference. There is hardly an indication to suggest I am at risk. I have little enough opportunity to explore the delights of London, and now you have curtailed my ability to do so further."

"If it makes you unhappy, I do apologize, but if it saves your life, I can hardly regret my actions."

She crossed her arms over her chest. "All this melodrama. Miss Harris was an assistant cook, and Miss Mansfield was training to be a seamstress. They were both working-class women, and it is likely their killer is from the same class."

His brows drew together sharply in disapproval. "Are you suggesting there cannot be a murderer in the higher echelons of the *ton*?"

Lizzy hesitated and then shrugged. "Perhaps, but it seems unlikely."

"Were you not the one who took me to task for excluding half the population from our suspect pool? Now you are doing the same based on class rather than gender. I am quite surprised at you, Miss Bennet."

She opened her mouth to retort, but Lizzy realized she had nothing to say. He made a valid point, so she grudgingly nodded. "I suppose you are right."

He feigned shock. Grasping his chest in a theatrical fashion, Mr. Darcy said, "I do not know if I can bear the shock of this moment. You are conceding I was right about something? That means you were wrong."

Her eyes narrowed as she glared at him. "I was possibly wrong. There is a difference, Mr. Darcy. You needn't act so ridiculous. I have never claimed I am always right."

His lips trembled with threatened laughter, as though he disagreed, but he apparently decided to stop teasing her. "If you will be arriving in the accompaniment of your aunt and uncle for the ball, I will not send a carriage for you, but I look forward to seeing you this weekend. If Mr. Kenton contacts me with any updates, I shall pass them along to you."

"That is the very least you can do since I am to be trapped here and unable to investigate on my own." Never mind she had already reached the reluctant conclusion there was little she could do to investigate Miss Mansfield's murder.

He gave her an indulgent smile, and she suspected if he'd been closer, he might've patted her on the head like a pup. She glared at him again as he stood up, inclining his head as he said, "I shall leave you for now, for I have things to which I must attend."

"It must be nice to have the luxury to leave."

He didn't bother trying to hide his chuckle that time as he turned and walked away. "Stay safe, Miss Bennet."

Since he wasn't looking at her, Lizzy felt it was harmless enough to stick out her tongue at him. It was perhaps the most juvenile of reactions, but satisfying, nonetheless. She was angry with him, but paradoxically, she was disappointed when he was gone.

Chapter Nine

Fitzwilliam hurried back to his townhouse, summoning his housekeeper and butler into the sitting room. He was surprised to find Charles waiting for him, but he had no time to dally at the moment. Instead, he said to Mrs. Harper, "We are hosting a ball this weekend."

The housekeeper's eyes widened. "This weekend, sir?"

"It will be a smaller affair than usual, but we will need to move quickly to make arrangements, and I shall task Georgiana with sending out the invitations." He spent the next few minutes discussing the semantics with his staff, and though he could see they were both daunted by the prospect of trying to make it all happen in a matter of days, he had every faith in their ability to do so.

Somehow, Charles had kept himself quiet during the conversation, but as Mrs. Harper and Mr. Williams departed, he grinned at Darcy. "How unlike you to throw an impromptu ball. It does go quite against convention for such short notice."

Grudgingly, Darcy sketched out the information for Charles, providing enough to explain why he felt moved to offer to host the ball for Miss Bennet. "It was an act of charity."

Bingley laughed at him, making no attempt to hide his amusement. "Of course, it was. It is simply an obligation you must undertake, and you have no desire to make the young woman happy." His tone was full of gentle mocking.

Darcy scowled at his friend. "Was there a reason you visited? Or are you simply here to entertain yourself at my expense?"

"That is undoubtedly an unexpected boon, but I did have a purpose. I wanted to prepare you, Darcy." Charles had turned unexpectedly serious.

Fitzwilliam sat down, realizing he was still standing after his conference with the housekeeper and butler, and he braced himself for whatever serious topic of conversation was on his friend's mind. He had no doubt it was connected to Miss Jane Bennet. "For what are you preparing me?"

"I intend to offer for Miss Jane as soon as I speak with her father." Charles said the words confidently, with no hint of defensiveness. He simply reflected firm resolve.

Recognizing that, Fitzwilliam knew it was useless to argue, but he still said, "I do not believe she holds you in high regard. Will you not at least consider the possibility she is more interested in your fortune than you?"

Bingley frowned, but he didn't exactly argue. "I did consider that possibility at your behest, and it was one of the reasons I agreed to leave Netherfield so hastily. I have discovered that time apart from Miss Jane has done nothing to impede my love for her, and I have pined for her. Before I learned Miss Jane was back in London, I had planned to return to Netherfield as soon as the weather permitted."

His eyes widened at the news, which Bingley had understandably not shared with him until this moment. "I see. Your mind is made up then?"

"Truly, it is. I do not believe it would matter to me if I discovered Miss Jane was more enamored with my fortune than me, but I assure you that is not the case. She is normally reserved, but when we are alone, she is completely different. I understand you have your doubts, and I wish to address them, but I also want to make it clear I will not tolerate disparaging talk of my future wife in days to come."

Darcy sighed regretfully. "I would not wish for this matter to end our friendship, so I will hold my tongue. I hope you are making the right choice and have properly evaluated Miss Jane's feelings for you."

"I have never been more certain of anything in my life."

He sounded entirely serious, which had the effect of slightly convincing Fitzwilliam. He had no doubt Charles believed what he was saying, though he still wasn't certain about Jane Bennet's feelings. It was different to see his friend so decided on a course, since Bingley tended to be more amiable and adapt to challenges in his path rather than try to stand fast against them. He must truly love Miss Jane, and Fitzwilliam hoped she loved him with equal fervor, for that was what his friend deserved.

"I do not expect you to offer congratulations, so I shall take your grudging silence in lieu." Bingley grinned then. "I would suggest a drink, but I suppose I should wait until I speak with Mr. Bennet before we celebrate."

Fitzwilliam smiled. "I doubt you shall have trouble gaining his agreement."

Mr. Bingley shook his head. "Indeed, I should not, for Miss Jane herself has told me she is definitely not his favorite daughter. The only one he is likely to object parting with is Miss Elizabeth."

That caused a jolt in Darcy's chest that he couldn't explain and didn't want to examine the reason for too closely. "Considering her sharp tongue and open dismissal of the state of matrimony, Mr. Bennet is likely to have her by his side for the rest of his life."

Mr. Bingley looked like he might challenge that for a moment, but at a warning look from Fitzwilliam, he closed his mouth. Fitzwilliam was in no mood to entertain discussion about his possible feelings for Elizabeth Bennet. His friend didn't know about his folly of proposing to her at Hunsford, and he intended to keep it that way. "I will try to keep an open mind and evaluate Miss Jane's behavior through the perspective you have shared, Bingley."

"That is all I can ask from you, along with maintaining silence if you still disapprove."

Fitzwilliam feared that would be even harder than reevaluating his opinion, but he nodded his agreement instead of arguing. His friendship with Bingley was one of the few he treasured in his life, and though he had tried to warn his friend, he could hardly force Bingley to forgo the woman who made him happy. He only hoped Miss Jane could make Charles as happy on a continuing basis as he appeared to be now.

SOMEHOW, THE STAFF and Georgiana had managed to throw together a ball that looked like it had been planned in detail, and at least eighty percent of their invitations had been accepted, so they had a respectable turnout. He was dismayed to see Mr. Elliott, Mr. Nobles, and Viscount Aumley in the assembly below as he stared down from the second-floor landing. He had deliberately left them off the guest list, but Georgiana must've added them.

Perhaps she thought she was doing something kind for Lizzy, having seen them interact before. He wanted to take his sister to task for that, but that would require a long and lengthy explanation of events he had no plan to relate to her. With a sigh, he accepted the damage was done, and the man was here now.

So was Lizzy, and he found it almost impossible to look away from her as she swept in on the arm of her uncle. Her aunt was on Mr. Gardiner's other arm, and Jane followed behind them with her gaze darting around the room. He doubted she was appreciating the ornate decoration of Darcy House's ballroom. Rather, she seemed to be looking for someone, and he was unsurprised when her gaze lit up upon falling on Charles Bingley, who was rushing toward them.

Fitzwilliam had a similar urge to rush down the stairs and greet them, but he forced his feet to remain where they were. It would be undignified to run toward them and act like an eager puppy, especially since he could well imagine how intolerable Lizzy would find the greeting. She seemed barely able to be in his presence, and he had difficulty seeing her again too. It was impossible not to relive the moment when he had made the fateful proposal that she had soundly rejected.

Even now, thinking about it made him squirm and shift in his dance pumps. He had taken a sensible and honest approach to the proposal, expecting Lizzy would've reacted in a similar fashion from what he knew of her. He had thought dispassionate logic and an acknowledgment of all the reasons why he shouldn't marry her but wished to anyway would have persuaded her to see his viewpoint. Instead, she had soundly rejected the proposal both because of its tone and because he refused to accept Jane loved Bingley.

That reminded him of his promise to his friend, and he tore his gaze from Lizzy, trying not to mind when Aumley almost immediately swept her into a dance, and kept his gaze on Jane as she interacted with Charles. He watched them from his perch on the second-floor landing as they danced for most of the first set.

He was reluctantly forced to admit he might've been wrong, and Jane's true feelings were revealed by the way she smiled at his friend, the angle of her head, and how closely she held her body to his whenever the opportunity presented itself. There was a difference in her expression and her overall manner when she was with Charles, and Darcy wasn't certain if she was just more secure in her emotions and was now showing them, or if he had been too blinded by his assumptions to see it before.

It was galling to admit he was probably wrong, but he was big enough to do so. He would need to tell Bingley that, but first, he wanted to make it clear to Lizzy he had realized the error of his ways. He owed her that, and it wasn't simply a bid to renew his marriage proposal.

He walked down the stairs and finally joined the party, mingling as he worked his way toward Miss Bennet over the next several minutes. She had danced a second dance with Lord Aumley, and he swooped in before someone else could entice her to dance the next set. Threading his arm through hers, he said, "Shall we get some air?"

She seemed surprised by his brazenness, but she didn't pull away. "I suppose that would be nice."

He led her to the balcony. It was a cold night, and normally, they would've hovered in the open doorway for a moment to refresh themselves, but instead, he pulled her out into the night air.

Lizzy immediately shivered. "I take it there is a reason you brought me out here?"

"Indeed, and it was not simply to freeze you."

Her lips twisted in what was clearly a reluctant smile. "Perhaps you would like to get on with it then?" She shivered again.

He thought about offering to hold her to share body heat, but he could well imagine how quickly she would reject the offer, no doubt outraged by the idea. Instead, he cleared his throat and said, "I believe I was wrong."

He had it coming, to be fair, when she grasped her chest in the same fashion he had affected the other day when she admitted she might not have been right. "Could it be, Fitzwilliam Darcy is admitting he was wrong about something?"

He took her response with good grace, waiting until her hand had returned to her side, and she seemed serious again before he said, "As I am no doubt wrong about a great many things in your eyes, allow me to clarify to what I refer. I believe I was incorrect in my assessment of Miss Jane's feelings. Having watched her with Bingley this evening, I can see she holds great affection for him. I have withdrawn any objections, and Bingley intends to speak with your father at the soonest opportunity."

Lizzy's eyes widened, and her lips parted on a gasp. For a moment, he had a difficult time tearing away his gaze from the plump contours, all too easily remembering how she tasted. That single kiss in his aunt's drawing room continued to haunt him to this day.

"That is wonderful news. I imagine he has already discussed it with Jane, but I shall not reveal the secret unless she speaks to me of it first, for I do not wish to ruin the surprise." She tilted her head. "How do you feel about the proposal?"

"I initially registered my reservations, but Bingley entreated me to revise my opinion with an open mind."

She scowled at him. "Of course, you can do that for Bingley, but when I ask you to, it is a Herculean task beyond imagining."

His lips pursed. "You needn't continue to remind me of my failings, Miss Bennet. I have admitted I was wrong, and I would expect you to accept that graciously rather than gloating or view it with resentment that I did not do so sooner."

"You may expect what you like, Mr. Darcy, but that does not mean you shall receive it." She spoke to him in that same too-sweet voice that had a way of needling him, but instead, he just laughed. Her disappointment was obvious.

"In light of my changed opinion, is it possible you might entertain giving me a second chance, Miss Bennet? Have I proven I am capable of revision and self-improvement?"

She hesitated for a moment. "You have proven that, but I fear it does not change anything, Mr. Darcy. We would be an incompatible match, and I am certain you must agree with that. We would argue far too often, and our values and worldviews are quite different. I appreciate you being able to reevaluate your opinion about Jane, but it can change nothing between us. For all I know, you are simply pretending to accept Jane as a way to soften my resolve."

He crossed his arms over his chest as he glared at her. "I resent that allegation. Have I ever lied to you, Miss Bennet?"

That she had to tip her head in consideration and clearly review their interactions irritated him, but eventually she shook her head.

"No, I do not believe you have ever been untruthful. Indeed, you are more likely to be honest to a fault, uncaring about the result."

He clamped his lips in irritation for a moment, not wanting the disagreement to escalate into a full-blown argument. "When I tell you I have reevaluated my opinion of Miss Jane, I am being sincere."

After a moment, she gave him a tremulous smile. "I thank you for that. It will make it easier for Mr. Bingley and for Jane. It will make it easier for us to meet with civility and accord in the future, for we are likely to be thrown together quite often with the joining of my sister and your best friend."

"But there can be nothing else between us?"

Once again, she hesitated, and she looked genuinely aggrieved when she shook her head. "I do not see how we could ever find true harmony."

"What about this?" As he said the words, he moved closer and put his hand on her cheek, gently urging her head backward. She complied without complaint, her lips parting before he even touched them.

The kiss was sweet and gentle, though it caused a flare of heat throughout his body. He kept it necessarily brief, fearing he would lose all sensibility if he continued to deepen it. Even the cold air would not be enough to distract him from the warmth he could find in her arms, and seducing her on a winter patio with his sister, friends, and members of the *ton* in the next room was beyond the pale. He took a step back. "Is there no accounting for the chemistry between us?"

Lizzy still looked sad. "I do not believe physical passion would be enough to sustain a marriage. Surely, it must fade at some point, and what would we be left with? You would regret lowering your standards to accept me, and I would surely regret allowing you to do so. Regret is no basis for marital accord."

He disagreed, certain the passion wouldn't fade, and also convinced they could build something more between them with the foundation they had, but he could see she was resistant to the idea. He hadn't given up, but he had to surrender for the evening.

He took a step back from her and gestured for her to precede him back into the ballroom, wishing he could call her back and persuade her there was a chance for them. He would have to regroup and figure out a new stratagem, because he didn't intend to give up when he was certain all chance of future happiness rested with Lizzy.

Chapter Ten

The ball was a success, and even in her unhappy state, Lizzy managed to have a good time. She had no end of admirers, and even though she and Mr. Darcy had parted ostensibly for good, at least in a romantic sense, she had even managed to dance with him in a polite fashion and interact as though nothing had changed, and they were merely acquaintances.

Jane was aglow with happiness, and it was clear Mr. Bingley had revealed his plan to her. She was discussing it on the carriage ride home, with Aunt Gardiner listening patiently, and Uncle Gardiner only grumbling a little bit about Mr. Bingley putting things out of order by not speaking with Mr. Bennet first before revealing his intentions.

"Do not fret so," said her aunt. "They are a modern couple, and times are changing, dear Edward."

Jane prattled on as though her uncle and aunt hadn't spoken, but she broke off abruptly when there was a cracking sound, and the carriage tilted precariously, landing heavily skewed to the right and leaning backward. "Whatever was that?" asked Aunt Gardiner, her panic clear.

"I believe we lost the axle," said her uncle. He was scowling. "Dreadfully expensive repair."

The driver appeared then, opening the door. "I am sorry, Mr. Gardiner, but the axle has broken, and I must ask all of you to step out of the carriage. It would be unsafe for you to remain in there while I see if I can repair the situation."

Lizzy followed the others exiting the carriage, climbing out awkwardly due to the angle. She was thankful to have her uncle's assistance, and she soon stood beside her family, lined up on the street.

"We have not traveled far from Mr. Darcy's house, and there were several hansom cabs waiting. I shall go flag us one," said her uncle.

Aunt Gardiner nodded as she huddled in her cloak. "I believe that would be a wise idea, dear. We shall all freeze if we remain standing out here for long."

Course set, Uncle Gardiner headed back toward Darcy House, while Lizzy, Jane, and her aunt huddled together for warmth. The poor driver was wrangling with the carriage, but Lizzy doubted he would be able to do anything. She moved a little closer to evaluate the damage, hoping it would be a simple repair the blacksmith could undertake, but as she drew closer, she was alarmed to find what appeared to be a clear cut on the axle.

Only the lower part had frayed, as though someone had sawed mostly through the wooden beam and waited for the last of the cracking to happen naturally. The damage could've been done days ago, or it could have been this evening, since it could likely be accomplished in a handful of minutes with a sharp saw. Whoever had done it, it seemed to be by design.

She shivered as she started to move back to her aunt and sister, wanting to warn them the accident was no accident. Before she could, a form coalesced out of the fog, grabbing her and clamping a cloth over her face. Before she could think better of it, she breathed in the sickly stench of chloroform and slumped against the man kidnapping her. She heard her aunt and Jane calling out, and they rushed toward her and her abductor, but he had shoved her into a carriage and was departing before they could catch up.

Lizzy was almost unconscious now, but she was alert enough to make out some of the features of the figure looming over her. Her mouth gasped in shock as she recognized Lord Aumley, and she had the disconcerting thought Darcy was going to gloat as she slipped into unconsciousness. She wondered with her last ability to think if Aumley intended to turn her into an oblation for Kali, since he was so enthralled by the mythology.

Chapter Eleven

Fitzwilliam paced around the drawing room, feeling uneasy for reasons he couldn't explain. The last of his guests had departed moments ago, and he should've been relaxing by now, but instead, he felt tightly wound. It was as though something was about to occur, but he couldn't imagine what.

He claimed no preternatural sensibilities, but it was almost no surprise when there was a frantic knock at the door, and he opened it seconds later to reveal Jane and her aunt standing there. He stepped aside so they could enter, picking up on their franticness. "What has happened?"

"Our carriage axle broke, and while Uncle Gardiner went to find a hansom cab, Lizzy moved closer to look at the damage. A form appeared out of the fog and kidnapped her. We tried to catch up, but we could not. We tasked the driver with following the carriage as far as he can while we came here to find my uncle and you."

Darcy, uncaring of decorum, bellowed, "Mr. Williams."

His butler hastily appeared, and if he thought less of Darcy for his display, he was wise enough not to show it. "Yes, Mr. Darcy?"

"Send someone to Bow Street for Runners. If possible, request Joseph Kenton. He is familiar with the situation. Mrs. Gardiner will remain behind to give the best directions she can while Miss Jane will come with me as we catch up with the driver."

"Very good, sir," said Williams, as though the kerfuffle happening was nothing worse than someone having received cold tea.

Darcy paused long enough to grab his greatcoat before following Jane out into the elements. He had not instructed Mr. Williams to send for his carriage, but he was unsurprised when it pulled up less than a minute later. The man was efficiency itself and was capable of sending for Runners and ordering the driver and carriage at the same time.

He opened the door, relaying the directions Jane provided so they were soon underway. They arrived at the site of the carriage accident a few minutes later, and Darcy had the driver stop for a moment because he saw a man stumbling around. He slid out of the carriage and rushed forward, recognizing Mr. Gardiner as he approached. The man was bleeding from his head and seemed confused, and Darcy led him to the carriage, helping him inside.

"What happened to you, Uncle Gardiner?" asked Jane with shocked concern.

"I do not entirely recall, my dear. I was walking toward Mr. Darcy's house when I believe someone thumped me on the head with a walking stick. That is all a bit vague and blurry though." He took the handkerchief Fitzwilliam extended, replacing the one he'd been holding to his head, since it was soaked with blood. "I do not recall much of anything past that."

"Which way did the thief's carriage go?" asked Darcy of Jane, not unfeeling toward Mr. Gardiner's plight, but also recognizing time was of the essence.

"To the right, Mr. Darcy."

Once again, he relayed the instructions to his driver and kept his head hanging out the carriage, intending to keep watch for the driver.

They caught up with the man within a couple of miles, and he looked winded, but he was still walking along at a rapid pace. He drew to a halt as the carriage stopped beside him, and he clearly recognized Mr. Gardiner, because he said, "My goodness, sir, what has happened to you?"

"There will be time for that later," said Darcy briskly. "Did you see where the carriage took her?"

The driver frowned, looking pained. "I did my best to keep up, sir, but I lost him a couple blocks back. It was a good thing he only had one horse on his carriage, or I would never have been able to keep pace for as long as I did. I do not know exactly where he took the young lady, but it has to be in this vicinity, likely near the wharf."

Fitzwilliam nodded his agreement as he departed from the carriage. "Continue to look for any sign of them. If you hear or find them, shout for help. I will be nearby, and there Runners *en route.*"

Jane leaned out the carriage window. "What are you doing, Mr. Darcy?"

"I intend to find Lizzy," he said with resolve, not waiting for her to register a protest if she intended to. There was nothing anyone could say to dissuade him from the course of action he'd set. He paused long enough to say, "I suggest you return either to Darcy House or the house on Gracechurch Street, Miss Bennet. It will be safer for you there, and Mr. Gardiner might need medical attention."

He didn't wait to see if they complied with his instructions as he started walking, cursing the blasted fog that made it almost impossible to see more than a few feet in front of his face. That the driver had maintained pace with the carriage for so long in these conditions earned the man an increase in salary, and Darcy made a mental note to suggest that to Mr. Gardiner once the crisis was over.

He felt like he'd been wondering aimlessly for hours, though it was probably only a few minutes, but it was seeming hopeless. Without a better lead on where she might be, he could stumble around near the wharf for hours, perhaps being impossibly close to her but never realizing it. His stomach clenched, and his chest compressed as he imagined what dreadful fate awaited her despite his proximity.

He was determined to find her, and he was starting to consider the possibility of pounding on every door until it yielded results when he heard a scream. It was quickly cut off, but he recognized Lizzy's voice as the one who'd uttered it, and it sent a chill through him when he raced in the direction from which it had come. He strained his ears, hoping she would cry out again to lead him, but at least he had a rough idea of where she was now.

Chapter Twelve

Lizzy woke with a pounding head, somewhat surprised to find she wasn't tied up or confined. Instead, Lord Aumley sat beside her on the bed, knife pressed close to her carotid artery. She turned her head and looked at him, her gaze still blurry, so it took her a moment to realize she had misidentified her kidnapper.

Instead of the viscount, his friend Mr. Nobles sat on the bed, and he was the one who held the pearl-handled stiletto to her throat. Her eyes widened, and she gasped with shock. "What are you doing, Mr. Nobles?"

"You called me Adam's name earlier," he said with amusement. "You even speculated I was sacrificing you to Kali."

Even in her befuddled state, Lizzy vaguely remembered the thoughts, but she hadn't realized she had uttered them aloud. "You do have a superficial resemblance to him."

"Perhaps more than superficial. I find it fascinating how many people can resemble others. For example, Miss Harris and Miss Mansfield both looked so much like my mother. My fiancée also reminded me of Mama. Dreadful, what happened to her." His words were sincere, but his eyes danced with lively mirth.

Lizzy shivered as he mentioned the two women who had been murdered, along with the fiancée she must presume he had also murdered, though surely had not decapitated. She had no doubt he was the one who had taken their lives, and there was also little doubt why she was here with him now. "Why would you kill them all if they reminded you of your mother?"

"Blythe Nobles was a capricious thing. Happy one moment and melancholy the next. I could never quite please her, but the few occasions when I came close were pure euphoria. But she was so exacting, demanding utter perfection and conformation." He sounded conflicted as he gave the account.

Lizzy licked her lips, confused what that had to do with anything, but unwilling to interrupt his rambling. It might lead to an enlightening discussion. More importantly, it might bring about a lapse in his concentration that would allow her a chance to escape. She had no idea by which means that might occur, but she wasn't ready to surrender to his nefarious intentions just yet.

"I loved my mother, but I was so angry with her. Always so angry, for there was no pleasing her. Try as I might, affect any change she wanted, and yet I was never good enough for her. How she preferred my dear sister to me." He looked morose.

"She was quite heartbroken when Beth fell through the ice. I thought after that, she would turn to me in comfort, but instead, she turned away. Her heart grew colder still, as though she were encased in ice beside Bethie. She was not the one who had fallen into the water and pounded so vigorously when she came up, clawing at the ice and pleading with her eyes for me to save her, yet she acted as though she had been the one to die too."

Lizzy shivered at what his words revealed. If he hadn't deliberately pushed his sister in through broken ice, he had at least stood over her and watched her try to escape without interceding. "That must have been difficult for you," she said softly, trying to sound compassionate.

He nodded. "Indeed. I did attempt to give her every consideration and every chance to change, but it never occurred. Alas, she was far too disappointing for me, as I was to her. It could not stand, but I learned one valuable thing from my mother."

Lizzy frowned, once again shuddering at his tone and his expression. It was genuinely chilling. "What did she teach you?"

"I learned from her the exquisite joy of stealing the life from a woman." He smiled as he said that, as though he had relayed his favorite brand of tea. "It is an incomparable experience to hold a woman's throat in your hands and squeeze until every vestige of life disappears from her gaze."

Lizzy whimpered slightly before stiffening her spine. She wasn't giving up yet. "If you prefer strangulation, why did you decapitate Miss Harris and Miss Mansfield?" How she sounded so cool and dispassionate, Lizzy wasn't certain, but she was proud of how calm she seemed. She certainly wasn't feeling it though.

"That was just a bit of fun after the fact. I toyed with the notion of framing Adam for the murders, since he is devoted to the Kali nonsense, and of course, I left Miss Mansfield at the park in hopes you would see my lovely gift. I might still frame Adam when I have finished. Once the Runners become aware of my activities, it will be much harder to carry them out, and I will be forced to change locations again. I am toying with the idea of going to the Colonies."

Lizzy couldn't help whimpering again. "How many places have you lived?" It was the closest she could come to asking how many victims he had, because she wasn't certain he would be blunt enough to give her a true answer.

"Four," he said, sounding slightly sad when he added, "My home village grew inhospitable shortly after my mother's death. I believe some of the people suspected me. They seemed to doubt my story that robbers had broken in to steal our possessions and killed her in the process."

"You indulge in your proclivities wherever you go?" Lizzy marveled that she could maintain the conversation, though she recognized she was clinging to it like a lifeline, and it was keeping her from descending into a hysterical mess.

"Of course. One can hardly be expected to give up their great passion."

She shifted slightly, and he pressed the blade closer to her skin with enough force for her to feel the tip, though it didn't cut her yet. "How many women have met their end at your hands?"

"Nine," he said like it was a trifling matter.

She frowned at him. "Does that count include your sister?"

He hesitated for a moment, tipping his head as though they were debating an academic matter. "I have considered including her in the count, but I am reluctantly forced not to do so. Her falling through the ice was strictly an accident of fate."

"I assume you stood over and watched her suffer though, making no move to assist her?" Her tone was neutral.

He appeared unaffected as he nodded. "It was quite revelatory. She was my first experience with death and watching the life fade from her eyes was quite pleasurable, but nothing compared to being the one to take it myself."

"You still contributed to her death, so I feel confident in saying you could add her to your tally." Lizzy couldn't believe the direction the discussion had taken, but she was happy to have anything to distract him.

"Perhaps. I shall have to give it more consideration. Truly, I am unlikely to reveal my number to anyone who will be around to recall it." He grinned at her, as though they shared a secret joke. "You are quite a good confidant, Miss Bennet, for you shall take any of my secrets to the grave."

"You do not have to do this. I barely know you, Mr. Nobles. I have done nothing that warrants your mistreatment." She narrowed her gaze. "I venture, neither Miss Harris nor Miss Mansfield did anything to provoke you either, nor your poor fiancée. I assume you noticed Miss Harris at the Perkins' party, but how did you meet Miss Mansfield?"

He gave an indulgent chuckle. "She was agog at the Dulwich Picture Gallery, and I impressed her with an observation. She accepted my invitation to tea at a nearby tearoom, and when the opportunity presented itself, I knocked her out and brought her to these rooms."

She shuddered. "So, the women did nothing to warrant murder?" How could anyone warrant the treatment he had dispensed was beside the point. She hoped to get him to see the flaw in his actions, but she doubted he was receptive to a logical discussion.

He seemed pensive for a moment. "No, I suppose not, other than bearing a strong resemblance to my mother. You look similar to her as well, Miss Bennet, and I was certain we would reach this point the very first night I saw you."

Hoping to delay whatever he planned, she asked, "How did you trick Marie into trusting you?"

"Marie was easy enough to lure away with a trinket, and when I did not try to seduce her that first evening, she assumed I was a gentleman. The foolish girl actually believed my tale of having fallen madly in love with her upon sight, and she agreed to run away with me to elope. I would have taken her that night, but we were interrupted, and she slipped from the carriage. She was quite disappointed to discover our destination was an entirely different sort when I retrieved her the next time."

He looked around the candlelit room, and there seemed to be a trace of affection in his expression. "It was in this very location where Miss Harris and Miss Mansfield met their ends as well. I have taken the rooms for a couple of months, but I will soon be departing London. You will likely be my last diversion in this space."

"Murder is quite a bit more than diversion," said Lizzy coldly.

"I can see where you might feel that way, since you have a different role to play than I do." He appeared gently amused, as though she were being ridiculous, and he was prepared to indulge it.

"What will you do to me?" Her eyes widened with horror as she contemplated the possibilities.

"I have already said that," he sounded impatient.

"Are you planning to violate me?" She sounded far calmer than she felt.

His expression twisted into one of disgust. "How dare you insult me in such a fashion? I would never stoop so low."

Lizzy's mouth dropped open in shock. He was clearly offended at the suggestion he might be a rapist, but he took being a murderer in stride. It was obvious he deserved a room in Bedlam, though she would be just as happy to see him confined to a cell at Newgate until the hangman's noose wrapped around his neck.

As she stared at him, Lizzy was certain there was nothing she could say or do to dissuade him from his actions. He was already too skilled at them, having committed nine-and-a-half murders before, if she only gave half-credit for his sister, so he was practically an expert at this. Having never been a homicide victim before, she was a novice, but she refused to surrender easily.

Knowing he would likely cut her the moment she opened her mouth, Lizzy still drew in a deep breath and let out a shrill scream for as long as she could until the knife nicked her skin, forcing her to fall silent.

He clamped a hand over her mouth and glared down at her. "You are ruining my fun, Miss Bennet. I see now I will have to gag you, though I do enjoy a bit of conversation first." He seemed resentful that she wasn't performing according to his mental script.

Lizzy wanted to keep fighting, but the blade was still against her skin, the stinging pain accompanied by a rivulet of blood dripping down her neck. She didn't think he had cut her fatally yet, but continuing to resist would likely lead to that outcome. Which did she prefer? Death by the stiletto or strangulation?

She was saved from having to make the decision by the door suddenly crashing open. She should've been surprised, but she wasn't at all when Mr. Darcy burst into the room in a spray of splintered wood.

Tristan's knife wavered for a moment, cutting her again, and she winced at the burn, but then he was pulled off her, and the two men engaged in a furious struggle. Lizzy considered trying to help, but she recalled the last time she'd interceded when Mr. Darcy was fighting with Mr. Wickham, and she'd accidentally hit him in the head with a tree branch, giving Wickham the inadvertent advantage.

She couldn't risk allowing that to happen this time, because she had no doubt Tristan would kill her and Mr. Darcy if he got the chance. Mr. Darcy might not be his type, but he wouldn't let that stop him.

She did scramble off the bed though, retrieving a handkerchief from her reticule he had left on the nightstand and pressing it to her bleeding wound as she watched the two men fight.

She had to concede Mr. Darcy was a skilled fighter, moving with lithe grace. She wondered if he had trained at Gentleman Jackson's. He didn't seem particularly vulnerable, even though she knew he had a tender spot his opponent could exploit.

There was a sudden cry of pain, and she darted forward before she could think better of it, unable to identify from whom it came for a moment as the two men slumped together. They fell to the floor, and she was certain Mr. Darcy was dead, her heart skipping a beat at the notion before pain constricted her chest to the point she could barely breathe. "Fitzwilliam, are you all right?"

"I am fine," he said a moment later as he pushed Tristan off him. He stood up, standing over the man who had his own knife sticking out his stomach. "He has not fared so well. With medical care, he will likely survive." Mr. Darcy sounded mournful of that idea, and he lifted his foot for a moment, it hovering over the blade of the stiletto. He seemed to be debating about whether he should push it in the rest of the way.

Lizzy, not wishing to see him reduced to that, moved forward and distracted him slightly from his thoughts, taking his hands. "You came for me."

He turned to face her, but his gaze remained on Tristan, who was huddled on the floor in misery. "Certainly, I did. Are we not partners in this venture?" He sounded calm and confident, but there was a tremble in his tone, and it turned to a full-body shudder when he saw the handkerchief pressed against her neck. "He has cut you?"

"He did so when I screamed, and then again when the door burst open." She pulled the handkerchief away slightly so he could see. "I do not believe it is a fatal wound, though I might need stitches."

He was pale, and when he pulled her into his arms, Lizzy didn't fight. Instead, she clung to him, taking warmth and comfort from his embrace. At that moment, all the things standing between them no longer seemed so important. Death had nearly cost them a chance at everything this evening, and what was pride when weighed against that?

Someone cleared his throat, and the two of them pulled apart as Mr. Kenton entered the room with a few other Runners behind him. "I assumed this might be the right place from the broken door," said the young man in a calm tone. He moved closer to Mr. Nobles, eyeing him with disdain. "This is our murderer, I take it?"

"He is," said Darcy confidently.

"I can attest to that," said Lizzy. "He confessed to nine murders. Ten if you count his sister, whom he failed to rescue despite being able to when she fell through the ice. The man killed his own mother."

Darcy paled further, likely realizing that a man who could kill his mother could kill anyone. Perhaps it reminded him how close he'd come to losing her, because his arms went around her again, pulling her against him, and he seemed uncaring that they had an audience who might disapprove of the close embrace between people who weren't married or even engaged. Lizzy didn't care either, and she curled closer to him, hugging tightly.

Mr. Kenton grimaced. "I suggest you see Miss Bennet home, for she is likely needing a surgeon. The lads and I can handle this. I shall need to conduct a more formal interview, but that can wait until morning."

"I believe he belongs in Bedlam," said Lizzy. "He seems quite mad."

Mr. Kenton nodded. "That might be his ultimate destination, but it is for others to decide after we present the evidence." He touched the brim of his hat in a respectful fashion as Fitzwilliam led her from the room.

Lizzy was happy to leave it all behind her, and as they stepped out into the foggy night, a wave of dizziness swept over her. She collapsed against Fitzwilliam, who lifted her into his arms and held her securely as the stinging in her neck suddenly became violent pain she could no longer ignore. She whimpered in distress, and it must have been more than Mr. Darcy could bear, because he went to the nearest horse tied to a hitching post, likely one who belonged to one of the Runners, and placed her on the saddle astride it.

She clung to the horn as he mounted behind her, putting his arm around her to hold her tightly against him when he started urging the horse to move faster and faster through the streets. They were probably going too quickly with the fog, but Lizzy was beyond issuing a warning.

Instead, she was trapped in pain and misery, and the events of the evening started to settle over her. Tears came to her eyes, and she trembled as she started to sob. Only his arm kept her tethered and focused, allowing her to keep from slipping completely into reaction from the overwhelming terror the evening had brought.

Chapter Thirteen

Lizzy somewhat recalled the journey back to the Gardiners', assuming Darcy had chosen that because it was closer than Darcy House. Otherwise, she wouldn't have been surprised to find herself instilled in his home, and indeed perhaps in his room, if he hadn't been thinking practically. A surgeon came, putting in four very painful stitches before departing, and Lizzy was left to rest, though Jane stayed with her.

She tried to fall asleep with little success, for each time she started to doze off, she was plunged into nightmares her mind conjured, various scenarios of the ways Mr. Nobles had killed his victims. When she woke from a dream where she had been trapped under the ice, pounding on it frantically as cold seeped into her body, she abandoned all attempt to sleep.

Jane was beside her in the bed, sleeping atop the covers and still in her ballgown. There was a chill in the air, so Lizzy took time to cover her sister before she left her room. She needed something to calm her nerves, and she was debating between warm milk and laudanum as she entered the sitting room.

She was afraid laudanum might trap her in the dreams, so she had discarded that notion when she drew to a halt at the sight of Mr. Darcy sprawled on the settee, his cravat loosened, his tailcoat stripped, and his waistcoat unbuttoned. He was in a state of dishabille, but there was something touching about it, and she moved closer.

She was unable to resist the compulsion to stand over him for a long moment and stare, memorizing his features. She had seen them many times before, but never in the unguarded state of sleep. It was only when she realized his eyes were pinched, and he seemed to be shifting restlessly that she grasped he might be having a nightmare as well.

Assuming he would appreciate being woken from such a state, after having been trapped in them for several hours herself, she leaned down and gently shook his shoulder. "Fitzwilliam, I believe you are having a nightmare."

His eyes snapped open, and he sat up immediately. In the process, he managed to knock her off balance, and she landed on his lap. She gasped at the contact, but there was no chance to escape as his arms came around her. He embraced her again, his relief tangible. She could hardly deny him the comfort, especially when she appreciated it herself, and she hugged him to her.

At some point, he must've found the fortitude to ease her back, because he gently lifted her off his lap and put her beside him on the settee, but still closer than was appropriate. His arm remained around her shoulders, and she rested her head against his chest, enjoying the sound of it thumping rhythmically under her ear.

"I thought I had lost you. That was intolerable, Lizzy."

She trembled. "I had the same thoughts, Fitzwilliam." How easily she had fallen into using his first name, as though it had always been a privilege open to her. She lifted her head to look at him, stricken by the sadness in his face. She raised a hand to touch his cheek. "I am all right. You saved me."

"I did not do it alone. If you had not had the courage to call out, I would not have found you in time."

Lizzy smiled at the concession. "I suppose I did my part. I even considered helping you by hitting him on the head with something."

His expression took on a state of mock-horror. "Never help me in that way again." He lifted a hand to rub his head, as though recalling the injury she had given him in the past.

His actions teased a smile from her, and she said, "I reached that decision on my own. I was afraid I would be hindrance rather than help."

"I am happy to have your assistance in many ways, but it is my duty to fight the villains on your behalf, Lizzy."

She rolled her eyes. "I do believe I could fight a villain on my own if I had to." Then reality returned, and she couldn't help remembering the feel of the knife sliding through her skin, which caused the wound to twinge. She quivered, and his arms went around her again. She pressed her face to his chest, though she wasn't crying this time. She was simply soaking up the succor he provided.

"You must know I love you, Lizzy."

She nodded her head, unable to look up to meet his gaze. Despite the events of the evening, she still had her reservations about a future being possible between them. Having nearly been separated from him was allowing her to reconsider some of her objections, but she was still uncertain they could be happy together in the long-term.

"Will you come to Pemberley?"

She lifted her head then, surprised by the question. "What?"

"I wish for you to come stay at Pemberley when the weather turns, and you can travel easily. I would like you to spend the spring with me. Of course, your family is welcome too."

Her eyes widened. "Even my mother?"

One of his lips curled into a slight smile, or it could have been a grimace of pain. It was difficult to discern. "Even your mother. Of course, your mother. Your sisters, your father, and the Gardiners as well, if they would like. You can bring anyone in the world you choose if it makes you feel comfortable enough to stay at Pemberley so we can get better acquainted. I would like to court you."

Lizzy licked her lips as she considered the idea. "What if I want to bring Lord Aumley?" she asked in a teasing fashion, hoping to distract him from the seriousness of the moment.

He scowled. "Anyone but him."

"He does not appear to be a rake," said Lizzy, unable to resist a little bit of torment directed toward Fitzwilliam. "It was his friend who was the murderer, not him."

"I made certain misjudgments about the young man, but he likes you far too much for my comfort. I am inviting you to Pemberley to have your undivided attention."

Lizzy abandoned her campaign of gentle teasing. "You do have my undivided attention, Fitzwilliam. I will come to Pemberley, and I will write to my mother this very night to tell her the news. Once she knows of it, there will be no rescinding the invitation or the acceptance."

His spine stiffened. "I shall prepare myself."

Her lips twitched, and she was unable to resist the compulsion to lift her head and brush them lightly against his. She wasn't certain if they could have a future together, but they definitely had a physical accord. Pemberley would allow them to see if they could build a true emotional accord as well. Though it had once seemed completely impossible, Lizzy found it probable now, and she was hopeful she could forge a future with Fitzwilliam. She was certainly willing to try.

This series needs to be read in order, just like Jane Austen's masterpiece.
The series in order:
Rapacity & Rancor[1]
Abduction & Acrimony[2]
Extortion & Enmity[3]
Murder & Misjudgment[4]

---

1. https://books2read.com/u/4ApM1d

2. https://books2read.com/u/mBwB1k

3. https://books2read.com/u/bxQGPe

4. https://books2read.com/u/bzZyAn

<u>Perfidy & Promises</u>[5]

PLEASE SIGN UP FOR Abbey's newsletter[6] to receive information about new releases. If you have any difficulties, email Abbey to request a manual add.

---

5. https://books2read.com/u/mddaAE

6. https://www.subscribepage.com/JAFF

About The Author

Abbey is a diehard Jane Austen fan and has loved Fitzwilliam since the first time she "met" him at age thirteen upon borrowing the book from the school library. He is the ideal man, though Abbey's husband is a close second. Abbey enjoys writing various steamy and sweet Jane Austen variations, but "Pride & Prejudice" (and Mr. Darcy) will always be her favorite.

Did you love *Murder & Misjudgment: A Pride & Prejudice Variation Mystery Romance*? Then you should read *Perfidy & Promises: A Pride & Prejudice Variation Mystery Romance*[1] by Abbey North!

Lizzy and her family arrive at Pemberley to allow Fitzwilliam a chance to court her. Things are off to a splendid start until Lady Catherine invites herself, and Caroline Bingley is clearly intent on causing trouble between ODC. Someone is targeting Fitzwilliam and Pemberley for harassment, but is it the same person who murders the stablemaster during Lizzy's stay? She and Darcy find themselves at odds over theories of the crime, but will that disagreement keep them from building a future together?

This is part five of the completed five-book "Crime & Courtship" series. They are intended to be read in order and follow roughly the same timeline

---

1. https://books2read.com/u/mddaAE

2. https://books2read.com/u/mddaAE

and locations as J.A.'s masterpiece. The first mystery takes place in Meryton. The next is at Netherfield, followed by Hunsford, then London, and finally Pemberley. The story arc continues throughout all five parts, compromising one long read broken into five sections. A mystery is central to each installment, so you could call this a cozy mystery sweet Regency romance.

While Abbey sometimes writes sensual JAFF, this series is strictly SWEET.

Also by Abbey North

A Month To Love
Reproach (Part One)
Resentment (Part Two)
Rapport (Part Three)
A Month To Love Compilation

Crime & Courtship
Rapacity & Rancor: A Pride & Prejudice Variation
Abduction & Acrimony : A Pride & Prejudice Variation Mystery
Romance
Extortion & Enmity: A Pride & Prejudice Variation Mystery
Romance
Murder & Misjudgment: A Pride & Prejudice Variation Mystery
Romance
Perfidy & Promises: A Pride & Prejudice Variation Mystery Romance
Crime & Courtship: A Sweet Pride & Prejudice Mystery Romance
Compilation

Darcy's Courtesan
Adversity (Darcy's Courtesan, Part One)

Avidity (Darcy's Courtesan, Part Two)
Amity (Darcy's Courtesan, Part Three)
Darcy's Courtesan: A Sensual "Pride & Prejudice" Variation

Marriage & Mysteries
Honeymoon & Hemlock

Mr. Darcy's Secret Stories
Mistaken Masquerade: A Pride & Prejudice Variation
Mischief & Matchmaking: A "Pride & Prejudice" Variation

Standalone
Christmas At Pemberley: A Pride & Prejudice Variation
A Scandalous Proposition: A Pride & Prejudice Variation
Shadow of Darcy: A Sensual Pride & Prejudice Paranormal Variation
Darcy's Obsession
Blackmailing Lizzy: A "Pride & Prejudice" Variation
Darcy's Wicked Game
Danger With Darcy: A Sensual "Pride & Prejudice" Variation
Passion & Prostrations: A Sensual "Pride & Prejudice" Variation
Darcy's Debt: A Sensual Pride & Prejudice Variation
Obstinacy & Obligation: A Sweet Pride & Prejudice Variation
Darcy's Alibi: A Sweet "Pride & Prejudice" Variation
Marooned With Darcy: A Sensual "Pride & Prejudice" Variation
Compromising Mr. Darcy: A Steamy "Pride & Prejudice" Variation
Marrying Mr. Darcy: A Sensual "Pride & Prejudice" Variation
Darcys' First Christmastide

www.ingramcontent.com/pod-product-compliance
Lightning Source LLC
Chambersburg PA
CBHW031426130726
47989CB00003B/1040